MESSENGER OF
FEAR

MICHAEL GRANT

First published in Great Britain in 2014
by Electric Monkey, an imprint of Egmont UK Limited
The Yellow Building, 1 Nicholas Road, London W11 4AN

Published with arrangement with HarperTeen,
a division of HarperCollins Publishers, Inc., 1350 Avenue of the Americas,
New York, New York 10019, USA

Text copyright © 2014 Michael Grant
Illustrations copyright © 2014 Joe McLaren

ISBN 978 1 4052 7682 5

A CIP catalogue record for this title is available from the British Library

Typeset by Avon DataSet Ltd, Bidford on Avon, Warwickshire

MIX
Paper from
responsible sources
FSC
www.fsc.org   FSC® C018306

EGMONT

Our story began over a century ago, when seventeen-year-old
Egmont Harald Petersen found a coin in the street. He was on
his way to buy a flyswatter, a small hand-operated printing
machine that he then set up in his tiny apartment.

The coin brought him such good luck that today Egmont has
offices in over 30 countries around the world. And that lucky
coin is still kept at the company's head offices in Denmark.

I normally dedicate my books to Katherine, Jake, and Julia. Not this time.

For Julia, Jake, and Katherine.

Because Julia is tired of always being named last just because she's the youngest.

1

My eyes opened.

I was on my back.

A mist pressed close, all around me, so close that it was more like a blanket than a fog. The mist was the color of yellowed teeth and it moved without a breath of breeze, moved as if it had a will.

The mist swirled slowly, sensuously, and it touched me. I don't mean that it was merely near to me and therefore inevitably touched me; I mean that it *touched* me. It felt my face like a blind person might. It crept up the sleeves of my sweater and down the neckline. It found its insinuating way under rough denim and seeped, almost like a liquid, along bare skin. Fingerless, it touched me. Eyeless, it gazed at me. It heard the beating of my heart and swept in and out of my mouth with each quick and shallow breath.

The mist spoke to me, wordless, soundless, and yet so that I understood, and it said, *Shiver.*

I shivered, and goosebumps rose on the insides of my arms and on my belly, and the mist laughed as silently as it had commanded me.

I called out, "Mom?"

But the mist would have none of that. It took my word, stopped it, flattened it, made a mockery of it, and echoed it back to me.

I felt something prickling and tickling the side of my face and turned my head to see that I was lying in grass of such a color that it could never have known spring. It was the gray-green of bread mold, the color of decayed life. I could see only the nearest stalks, those pressed closest to my face. How had I come to be here? And where was *here?*

I searched my memory. But it was a box of old photos printed on age-curled paper. Here a face. There a place. Not quite real, too faded, too fractured, too far away to be real. Pictures, snatches of conversation, distorted sounds, and sensory echoes—the soft scraping sound of paper pages turned by an unknown hand, liquid poured from a bottle, the strike of a match, the smell of sulfur, the—

I had the thought then that I was dead.

It was not a certainty to me but an uneasy possibility, a doubt, a guess whose truth I was not willing to test.

Why were my memories so far out of reach? I had a life, didn't I? I was a person. I was a girl. I had a name. Of course I had a name.

Mara.

Yet even that seemed unsteady to me—a fact, perhaps, but a shaky fact. The word *Mara* did not carry with it some flood of emotion. It was a flat thing without depth or shape, just a word.

Mara.

Was that me? Let it be me. Let it be me because I needed a name, I needed something definite to hold on to.

I raised a hand to my face. I watched the fingers appear, swirling through that unnatural mist. I touched my face and felt tears. I touched my face and *felt*. Both finger and cheek felt and therefore I lived. I lived.

Then, as if discouraged by my discovery, the mist began to clear. It withdrew from me, sliding away from my flesh like a wave retreating into the sea.

I wanted to stand up. I did not want to lie there any longer in the dead gray grass. I wanted to stand and see, and then run, run far from this unsettling nightmare. Running would awaken me, and all of it, all my memory, all that I was would come flooding back. It must.

I was shaking so badly that the simple act of standing erect became a challenge. My limbs did not want to cooperate with each other, and I made a mess of it, rising first onto hands and knees and then stumbling, nearly falling, before finally rising to my full unimposing height.

I was in an open place. It was dark, darker than it had been in the mist, and no starlight, still less moonlight, shone down from above. But it was not complete darkness. Patterns of gray on black, and black

4

on blacker still, emerged as I looked around me.

There was a building. Had it been there the last time I looked? No light escaped that building. Nothing about that building called to me to approach except for the fact that it was the only object in sight.

I moved one foot, and another. That fact, the fact that I could put one foot in front of another, let me take a deeper breath, a less agitated breath. To move was to live, wasn't it? To move was to choose a path, and that meant I still had some volition, some control. I felt and I moved. Hadn't there been some lesson in class about the definition of life and hadn't it been that . . . sensation, movement, something else . . .

Had there been a class? A school?

Of course, no doubt. So why couldn't I see it in my mind? Why, when I asked myself that question, was the only image like a stock photo, filled with unfamiliar, too-bright, too-pretty faces?

Was I dead?

Never mind, Mara, I told myself, trying to accept

that name as the truth. Never mind, *Mara*, you can feel and you can move. You can choose. *Mara*.

I could go in a different direction. I could choose not to walk to that building, that outline of black against black, that shadow within shadow. My feet made sounds like sandpaper as they brushed the brittle grass.

The structure was taller than a house, narrow and long. There was a suggestion of high windows ending in pointed arches. And a suggestion, too, of a strong, heavily timbered door, and above that door, atop the building, a sort of tower.

A steeple.

It was a church. That knowledge should have reassured me, but instead it drove a spike of cold terror into my belly, for I knew one thing: this church was no place of comfort and peace. There was a sullen, silent hostility to this structure. It was not calling me into God's presence; it was warning me to go away.

Yet at the same time I could now feel the door drawing me to it. It had a strange gravity, a force perhaps unknown to science that pulled me toward it not by magnetism but by acting on my fear, turning my fear into a vortex. I had to know what was inside that church. I had to know, though I feared the knowing.

You fear me, come to me, the church seemed to whisper to my heart. *Your terror demands an answer. Come.*

Come.

And flee.

I reached the door. There was a brass doorknob, strangely shaped, as though it was a carved figure. A head, perhaps. I touched it and my curious fingers could make nothing of the curves and ridges, though I thought I might almost make out the outlines of a face.

I turned the knob and it moved easily. I pushed open the door. An answer was close now, I felt, some piece of knowledge that I both dreaded and desired.

I stepped across the threshold and glanced up, sensing something overhead, and where I thought I would see rafters, there was the sickly mist again, a shapeless carrion feeder greedily awaiting my death.

I moved down the aisle, like a bride slow-walking between rows of family and admirers. There was no altar or cross or other symbol. There was only an oblong box set upon a low stone so that the top of the box would be just lower than my breast if I were to stand close.

It was a *coffin*.

Something told me it was not empty.

I was sure that I would see a familiar face in that coffin. I was sure I would see myself. But why would I be lying in a church that was no church?

Cold fingers of horror squeezed my heart, wrung the blood from it, and left me gasping for air. Each inhalation was a sniffle, each exhalation a shudder. My fingernails pressed into my palms, and the pain of it was proof that I was alive, or something like alive, and yet I knew, I knew what I would see in that coffin.

I took another step.

Another.

And I looked down to see a face.

I stared in confusion. This was not me. Could not

be me. I could not bring the image of my own face to mind, yet I knew this was not me.

Maybe she had been fifteen years old, maybe a year older; it is not easy to judge the age of a dead face. My age, perhaps?

That she was dead was not in doubt.

"Her name was Samantha Early."

A voice!

I spun around, raising my hands—already formed into aching fists. Adrenaline chased away the lethargy of dread as instinct took over.

He was a boy or young man. He stood a dozen feet away and did not move toward me or flinch at my upraised fists.

He was tall and thin. His face was pale as a ghost, pale almost to translucence, and made all the whiter by the long black hair that framed it.

He wore a black coat that fell to mid-calf over an iron-gray buttoned shirt. His pants were black, and his shoes seemed to be tall boots of black leather, though they were dusty. The buttons of his coat were silver but not brightly polished. Each was a tiny skull, no bigger than a hazelnut.

On his right hand was a silver ring in a shape I could only vaguely make out. It looked like a warrior, a woman, gripping a sword.

The other ring, the one on his left hand, was a face contorted in unimaginable terror. A young face, and in between nervous glances it seemed to change, as though the face was animated, alive.

I had as well the impression of tattoos at wrist and neck, from the few visible patches of skin.

His eyes were the only color in that monochromatic picture. They were blue. They were a blue I had never seen before in any human eye. His eyes were the turquoise of the Mediterranean, like something from a travel poster of a Greek island.

I wanted to ask him where I was, but that would have made me seem vulnerable. It would have invited him to take some advantage of me. Better to be tough, if tough was something I could pull off. So instead I asked the question that was inevitable.

"Who are you?"

He looked at me and I had to force myself not to turn away. He looked at me and I felt quite exposed suddenly, as if his eyes were seeing the things I showed no one. I fought an urge to squirm, but still my shoulders hunched forward, and my eyes lowered, and my lips pressed tightly and my lungs labored to take in breath so that my nostrils flared.

All of it was beyond my ability to control.

"Her name was Samantha Early. It is a terribly apt name. Dead too early is young Samantha Early."

Was I supposed to laugh? Was that some effort at a joke? But nothing about him suggested humor.

"Tell me who you are," I said. My voice sounded pitifully thin. If there was any threat in that voice, then it was a laughable one.

"That's not the question you want answered first," he said.

MICHAEL GRANT

He had a strange voice. It was as if his mouth was pressed close against my ear so that I could hear every shade of every word, the inhalation and exhalation, the play of tongue against teeth, teeth against lips, lips softly percussing the *b* and *p* sounds.

I recoiled a bit from that voice, not from fear but from a sense that its intimacy was somehow inappropriate.

"Are you reading my mind?" I asked.

There was the slightest narrowing of his eyes, and if not a smile, there was a softening of the stern lines of his mouth.

He did not answer. Instead he said, "Samantha Early. Aged sixteen. Dead by her own hand."

With that he laid his pale fingers softly, reverently on her cheek and then rolled her head to the side so that I could see.

"Oh, God!" I cried. It was a hole, just large enough that a little finger could have been stuck into it. The hole was in her temple, and it was the color of ancient

12

rust. Around the hole, an elongated oval of scorched skin and crisped hair.

It was the most terrible thing I had ever seen in my life.

I looked then at her face. She was not pretty; her chin was too big, too meaty. Her nose was perhaps too forceful, and there were dark circles under her eyes. I felt, seeing this face, that she had endured pain. It was a sad face, though how can a face in death ever be happy?

I was so intent on her face that I failed at first to notice that the light all around me had changed.

I looked up and saw that the church was gone. The coffin, that terrible object, that reproach against life itself, grew transparent.

And then, the pale flesh of the dead girl began to regain some aspects of life. It grew pink. And I was certain I detected the movement of her eyes beneath their lids.

I cried out, "She's alive!"

And just then, as though my exclamation was a

signal, she sat up. She sat up and now, dreamlike, the coffin was no longer there. Feeling wildly unstable, I put my hand out as though to steady myself, but there was nothing within my reach but the shoulder of the boy in black.

My fingers closed around his bicep, which flexed at my touch. It was reassuring in its solidity. He was real, not some figment.

He shook his head and did not meet my eyes. "I am not to be touched."

It wasn't anger but a soft-spoken warning. It was said with what might have been regret but with absolute conviction.

I pulled my hand away and mumbled an apology, but I was less concerned about him than I was consumed with the horror of looking directly into the dead girl's eyes. She had risen to her feet. She stood. The hole still a testament to brutality, bloody, only now, now, oh . . . oh . . . It was *bleeding*. Wet and viscous, the blood drained from the hole in her head as the blood seemed to drain from my own limbs. Little globules of something more solid slid down the trail of blood, bits of her brain forced outward as the bullet had forced its way inward.

Her eyes were brown and empty, her face blank, her blond hair fidgeted in a slight breeze, and the blood ran down her cheek and down her neck and pooled at the hollow of her throat.

I wanted to say that we needed to call 911. I wanted to say that we must help. But the boy in black stood perfectly still, looking at me and not at the girl, the girl dead or living or whatever unholy cross between the two that defined Samantha Early.

Dead too early.

"The question you want answered," the boy in black said as though no time had passed, "is whether *you* are dead."

I licked my lips nervously. My throat burned as though I'd been days without a drink of water. "Yes," I said to him.

"You live," he said. "She does not."

2

"We have to help her."

"She is past help," the boy in black said.

"She's standing, she's . . . Can you hear me?" I addressed this to Samantha, knowing how foolish it was, knowing that my words would fall into the inconceivably vast chasm that separates the living and the dead.

No flicker of recognition in those brown eyes, no sudden cock of the head. I was inaudible and invisible to her.

Then she began to move, to walk. But backward. Away from us but backward, not awkward but with normal grace. As though she had always walked backward. Backward across what was now a suburban street. A car came around the corner, not fast, the driver seeming to check for addresses as he drove. If he saw

Samantha, he gave no sign of it. I was sure, too, that he did not see me or the boy in black.

The car moved forward normally. Across the street a dog raced along its enclosure, moving forward as well, seeing the car but not us. Only Samantha was in rewind, only she moved backward to the sidewalk, to the flagstone-paved path, to a front door that opened for her. Now it was opened *by* her but all in reverse. It was a disturbing effect, part of what I was now sure had to be a strangely elaborate dream. Dreams could play with cause and effect. Dreams could show you bullet wounds and staring girls and people walking backward. Dreams could move you from black-hearted un-church to sunlit suburbia without effort.

"A dream," I whispered. I looked again at the boy. He had heard me, I was sure of that, but his expression was grim, focused on Samantha.

The door of the house closed and should have blocked her from our view, but we were now inside that house, though we had passed through no door. We were in a hallway, at the foot of steps leading upward.

There were framed photos on the wall beside the steps: a family, parents, a little boy and Samantha. And other pictures that must have been grandparents and aunts and cousins. I saw them all as, without thinking about it, I began to ascend those steps. Even as Samantha walked backward up them.

She disappeared around the corner at the top, but the boy in black and I arrived at her room before she did. By what means we came there, I could not say, except that that's how dreams are.

I felt sick in my stomach, the nausea of dread, because now I was sure that I knew what terrible event I would soon witness.

And oh, God in heaven, if there is one, oh, God, it was happening, happening before my eyes. Samantha sat on the edge of her bed. The gun was in her lap. Tears flowed, sobs wracked her, her shoulders heaved as if something inside her was trying to escape, as if life itself wanted to force her to her feet, force her to leave this place, this room, that gun.

"No," I said.

She was no longer moving backward.

"No," I said again.

She raised the gun to her mouth. Put the barrel in her mouth. Grimaced at the taste of steel and oil. But she couldn't turn her wrist far enough to reach the trigger and yet keep the barrel resolutely pointed toward the roof of her mouth.

She pulled it out.

She sobbed again and spoke a small whimper, a sound so terrible, so hopeless, and then she placed the barrel against the side of her head, which now no longer showed the wound, the wound that was coming if she didn't—

BANG!

The noise was so much louder than in movies. I felt as if I'd been struck physically. I felt that sound in my bones and my teeth, in my heart.

Samantha's head jerked.

Her hand fell away, limp and blood-spattered.

Blood sprayed from the hole for a moment, then slowed to an insidious, vile pulsation.

She remained seated for a terribly long time as the gun fell and the blood poured and then, at last, she fell onto her side, smeared red over the pastel floral print of her comforter, and rolled to the floor, a heap on the carpet.

The gunshot rang in my ears. On and on.

"I don't like this dream," I said, gritting my teeth, shaking my head, fighting the panic that rose in me.

The boy in black said nothing. He just looked, and when I turned to him for explanation, I saw a grim mien, anger, disgust. Simmering rage. His pale lips trembled. A muscle in his jaw twitched.

He crossed abruptly—his first sudden movement—to the desk in the corner of the room. There was a laptop computer open to Facebook. There were schoolbooks, a notebook, a Disney World cup holding pencils, a dozen colorful erasers in various shapes, a tube of acne medicine, a Valentine's card curled with age, a photograph of Samantha and two other girls at a beach, laughing.

There was a piece of paper, held down at the four corners by tiny glass figures of fancifully colored ponies. The paper had been torn from the notebook.

The boy in black looked down at the paper and said nothing. He looked at it for far longer than it could have taken to read the few words written there in blue ink. I knew, for I, too, read the words.

I love you all. I am so sorry. But I can't anymore.
—Sam

I found that I could not look up from the words. I felt that if I looked away, I must look at the dead girl, and I didn't want to see her. She had still lived when she had written these words.

Then I realized that he was looking at me.

"Why is this happening?" I asked him.

He touched the note reverently with one finger.

"Why am I here?" I asked with sudden vehemence.

"The same reason we are all here," the boy said. "To learn."

But I had lost patience with cryptic answers. "Hey. Enough. If this is a dream, then I don't have to put up with you!"

"Mara," he said, though I had never told him my name. "This is not a dream."

"Then what is it, huh?" My voice was ragged. I was sick through and through, sick with what I had just witnessed, sick with what I feared about myself. "What is it and what are you?"

"I am . . ." he began, then hesitated, considered, and again showed that slight lessening in the grim lines of his face. "I am the messenger."

"Messenger? What's your message, showing me this poor dead girl? I never wanted to see that. I don't want it in my head. Is that your message? Showing me this?"

"My message?" He seemed almost surprised by the

23

question. "My message? My message is that a price must be paid. A price paid with terror."

I reached to grab him angrily, but he moved easily out of range. I had wanted to grab him by the throat, though I had instead reached for his arm. It was not that I blamed him for what I was now enduring, it was rather that I simply needed to hurt someone, something, because of what I had seen, and what I had felt since waking to find myself in the mist. It was like an acid inside of me, churning and burning me from the inside.

I wanted to kick something, to shout, to throw things, to scream and then to cry.

To save that poor girl.

To wipe the memory from my mind.

"You're the messenger?" I asked in a shrill, nasty, mocking voice. "And your message is to be afraid?"

He was unmoved by my emotion . . . No, that's not quite right. It was more accurate to say that he was not taken aback. He was not unmoved, he was . . . pleased. Reassured?

"Yes, Mara," he said with a sense of finality, as though now we could begin to understand each other, though I yet understood nothing. "I am the messenger. The Messenger of Fear."

It would be a long time before I came to know him by any other name.

Calmer now, having released some of my boiling anger and worry, I turned my unwilling eyes back to Samantha Early. Her life's blood was running out, soaking into the carpet.

"Why did she do it?" I asked.

"We will see," Messenger said.

3

Samantha Early looks at the clothes hanging in her closet. She clenches her fists. The veins on her forearms stand out. Her body seems to vibrate with tension.

I see this. It is happening. I can neither look away nor remain indifferent. Messenger has shown me the outcome, so I cannot tell myself that all I am witnessing is teen angst.

By means I can neither explain nor ignore, I know her thoughts. I know what she feels as she gazes, frightened, frightened by nothing but a closetful of clothing.

What will not draw ridicule? That is the question she asks herself. She dresses defensively: What will avoid giving anyone an excuse to ridicule? It should have been easy, getting dressed. It should have been as simple as what top goes with which jeans or shorts or skirt, no, no, not skirt.

No, not skirt. She remembers that day when she tripped in a skirt, when she'd sprawled out across the hallway, finger still stuck in the loop of her locker's combo lock, books strewn out into the path of oncoming students, who stepped aside indifferently or made a show of it, made a thing of it and laughed.

Spazmantha.

Not even original, that. She had first heard Spazmantha when she was eleven.

It shouldn't bother her. She knows that. Her mother has told her that. Her shrink has told her that. Actually, the shrink said, "You have bigger issues than that to concern yourself with."

How do I know this? How am I seeing this? This dream is a very strange movie in which I watch Samantha and watch her thoughts at the same time.

The shrink's bigger issue was obsessive–compulsive disorder. OCD for short. Everyone threw that term around like it was nothing, like it was cute, OCD. "Yeah, I'm a little OCD? Hah hah." It wasn't cute, and Samantha did not have a little of it.

Samantha goes to the bathroom and washes her hands. She uses Cetaphil soap because it's mild, but she uses a brush as well, a wooden-handled bristle brush. First, the hot water. Then the Cetaphil, taking care that every single square inch of her hands—and for purposes of her compulsion, her hands end at the first crease in her wrist—is covered. Then the brush. She brushes hard. Then she rinses.

And that's one.

I watch as Samantha begins the process all over again. The Messenger stands behind her. Samantha sees neither of us. This isn't happening, this has *already* happened. The Samantha movie is in a flashback.

"Can she hear us?" I ask, but the answer is obvious: Samantha can neither see nor hear us. She is washing her hands, has already washed her hands, done all this already. I'm seeing it, here, in my present, but it's in the past.

I can smell the soap. I feel the steam rising from the

too-hot water. When I step to one side, I can see myself and Messenger in the mirror.

He's taller than I am. He's white, I'm Asian. He's . . . beautiful? I'm . . . pretty? Maybe that, maybe pretty, but not beautiful. I'm not sure many girls could call themselves beautiful while sharing a mirror with Messenger.

There's something about him that seems unnatural. He's a marble statue brought to life, unreal. Isn't he? He can't be real, not really real, if for no other reason than no one dresses that way. And yet there is a weight to him, like a distortion of gravity, a bending of light, as if he was made of the stuff of collapsed stars.

I force my gaze from him and back to a more distressing vision: Samantha Early begins a third round of washing. Her hands are obviously spotless—she could perform open heart surgery without wearing gloves—yet, caught in the compulsion, she washes her hands a fourth time. The backs of her hands are bright-pink now, like sliced ham, with fingertips so raw that the cuticles are tearing away in tiny shreds. She wields the brush with a ferocity that is necessary to her, energy that she must expend, pain that she must endure.

On the fifth washing little drops of blood ooze from the cuticle of her ring finger.

"Can't she stop?" I ask.

"If she fails to wash her hands seven times, her family will die," Messenger says.

"What?" I snap. "That's crazy."

"Compulsion is very like insanity," Messenger says.

He is not indifferent, that's the thing. His too-near voice that seems always to be whispering in my ear is held to a standard of cool detachment, but his eyes and his mouth and his forehead and the way he swallows all speak of reflected pain.

He understands. He feels. I'm convinced of that at least. There's a humanity to him. He's not entirely cold and beautiful and strange—there's something of flesh and blood there as well. That reassures me. He may be only a figment of a dream I'll forget upon waking, but still I am relieved.

It *is* still a dream. What else could it be? I wake in a field with a mist covering me, and then, all of this?

Wait, had I fallen asleep? I try to recall, I strain to dredge some memory out of my foggy brain. But again it is as if all I can see of my waking life is a sort of clip-art version, a stock photo version with generic people acting generically, none of it possessing the detail and grain of reality.

Samantha begins her sixth round.

"Is this why—"

"Many things are *why*," Messenger says. "But this is for our deeper understanding."

Why do we need to understand? I want to ask him that, I want to demand an answer to that, because there has to be some very good reason why my subconscious mind would lay these sad images before me like a fortune teller laying out her tarot cards. But all of Messenger's answers were vague, and after all, was there a point in asking why within a dream? Eventually I would wake up, and then I could consider the meaning of it all. Calmly, coolly, with the sick sadness of it all pushed aside and relabeled as nothing more than random imagery conjured from an overtired mind.

We were no longer in Samantha's bathroom. We were at a school. But not my high school; of that I was sure. Almost.

A banner on the wall of the corridor read CARLSBAD HIGH SCHOOL—GO SPARTANS. The colors were maroon and gold. The colors at my school were . . .

What were they? I was sure I was in high school, and sure that this was not it. Why couldn't I remember my school colors?

Dreamland was a strange world where cause and effect could be reversed, where one could move effortlessly from place to place. Where gaunt, beautiful boys with intimate voices and eerily blue eyes could wear skulls for buttons. Yes to all of that, but if this was a dream, shouldn't I be able to recall my school colors? Or my name?

Mara? Mara *what*? I felt the knife's edge of panic

again. If I stopped believing this was a very lucid dream, if I started for even a moment to believe this was real, I would have to be afraid, and I feared that moment when I might be forced to cross the line into a more personal terror.

Samantha's hands were pink and torn, but they were very clean as she walked down the hallway, thinking to herself that there was more to life than this place, that she would be out of this place soon.

"I know what she's thinking," I said, walking behind Samantha with Messenger just a pace behind me.

"Yes," Messenger said, and that voice carried notes of warning coiled within the single syllable.

Samantha had spotted someone in the crowd ahead of her. I knew the name: Kayla. Kayla McKenna. K-Mack, some people called her, and it was like a brand name. It meant more than this one tall, willowy blond girl alone; K-Mack meant a group. K-Mack meant a power within the school. A force.

Kayla was more than pretty. Kayla had large brown

eyes framed by absurdly long lashes. She had perfect cheekbones. Her every movement was graceful and assured. She was dressed impeccably. Her hair tumbled, liquid, like honey, like something out of a shampoo commercial. Her skin was flawless, untouched by blemish.

Samantha instinctively put a hand to her face, traced her finger over the bump that had begun to emerge just beside her nose, a zit in the making.

Having touched it once, Samantha had to touch it twice more. Three times touch. Or something awful would happen, something unspeakable.

Kayla was surrounded by people. Three girls and two boys. Certainty and smugness oozed from them all, but they were planets circling Kayla's sun.

"Stop touching it, Samantha," Kayla said. She had an interesting way of inflecting, Kayla did. The "touch" part of "touching" was punched with a humorous uplift. Like the word itself was funny.

Samantha's hand froze in place. Kayla had disrupted

the count, and now she would have to do it again. Three times.

"It's just a zit," Samantha said, and touched it.

"Yeah, I didn't think it was a unicorn," Kayla said. The emphasis on "didn't", with the same comical uplift. "Oh, my God, you're *touch*ing it again. Stop *touch*ing it! You're making me sick, honestly. No offense."

The way she spoke was an invitation to a conspiracy —it invited all to see the humor, all to see that she was just joking, just having fun. Her eyes mocked, but was there anything to point to as proof that she was aware of the effect on Samantha?

"No offense," Samantha echoed, and smiled a sickly smile and strained with all her will to keep her hands at her sides, not to touch.

All of them were looking at her now, the K-Mack crowd, staring at her, expectant, waiting on the signal to laugh at her.

"How's your . . . um . . . book coming?" Kayla asked. The word "book" got the uplift this time, in a way that clearly cast doubt on the possibility that there was such a book.

"Okay, I guess. I have to get to class."

"Aren't you done writing it? You said in Mr. Briede's class you were done."

Samantha fought down a wave of anxiety. Mark Briede was the teacher who had most encouraged her to write. But she didn't want to talk about the book, or think about the book, or think of how she wanted to touch her face. She had to begin the count again, had to make it three times. The book was just stupid. She would probably just be a huge failure—what were the odds of some sixteen-year-old girl publishing anything?

And if she did? She had revealed bits of herself in the story. One of the characters would be blindingly obvious as herself, as a prettier, cooler Samantha, an aspirational Samantha. She would make herself even more of a target, she would have painted a bullseye on herself . . . No, a targeting map, like the military used. *Strike here and here and here to inflict maximum damage.*

"I'll see you guys later," Samantha said, and fled, touching her bump. Touching it. Touching it again. Relief.

I looked at Kayla rather than Samantha now.

"Is she doing it on purpose? Does she know she's being cruel?"

"Is that important?" Messenger asked.

"Yes," I said.

"Listen to her thoughts," Messenger said.

And I heard them. Kayla's thoughts. As clearly as if she was speaking. In fact, when I looked, I saw her lips moving. She was speaking but not to the others around her. It was more as if I'd given her a truth serum that caused her to explain herself honestly.

"I don't like Samantha. She's very smart, but so am I. And I'm prettier by a mile and also much more popular. I pick on her because she's weak. It's that simple. She's obviously got problems, so anything I say can make her freak out."

It was bizarre the way Kayla spoke, unsettling even by dream standards. She wasn't looking at me—she wasn't looking at anyone—she was just voicing her thoughts, like I'd thrown a switch just by wondering about her. She was Richard the Third in Shakespeare's play, pausing for a moment to enlighten the audience as to motive and malice.

"Why shouldn't I pick on Samantha? It's fun for me and entertaining for my friends. It reminds my friends to be a little afraid of me, and that's useful. It reminds them that they could be next if they disappoint me. Besides, I can't stand that she—"

She stopped just like that, in mid-thought.

I laughed. Not because it was funny but because it had the ring of truth and I had not often heard truth spoken so bluntly and so utterly without self-justification.

I turned my laughing face to Messenger, who was watching me, waiting for my reaction. Judging me, I thought.

"If this is a dream, why aren't we at *my* school?" I asked him. "I should dream about places I know. This place probably isn't real."

He must have heard the uncertainty in my voice. I did.

"Okay, that's enough," I said sharply. "I want answers. I want to know what this is." The panic came quick and strong, all at once, catching me by surprise. "This is real, isn't it? This is real. Oh, God, this is real. This is real!"

"Bravo! Well done. She's not nearly as thick as you were, Messenger." A female voice. Not Kayla. Not Samantha, who was all the way down the hall now and entering a classroom.

Kayla's little group broke up as the bell rang with startling urgency, and, just like it was at my school when the bell rang, the hallway emptied out fast, the last stragglers rushing away with backpacks swinging.

The girl who had spoken, well, maybe she was a girl physically and chronologically but surely not psychologically. No girl could have carried herself this way. A woman, then. A young woman to look at but with no hint of youthful innocence.

She was as pale as Messenger and, like him, dressed in black. But this girl/woman had a great deal less clothing in total. She wore a thing that was a cross between a bustier and a leather jacket. Cutouts revealed her shoulders, the neckline plunged to her breastbone, and the whole garment was cut to a severe point in front, forming a V that hid her navel but left the sides of her waist and her lower back bare. She wore black tights that seemed more liquid than fabric and swirled with black-on-black patterns that shifted and changed. Her boots went to her knees and were notably strange for suggesting that her feet were unnaturally small.

That detail bothered me, held my attention for a moment, as I could not see how she could stand on such tiny feet, particularly given the height of the heels.

If Kayla was the blond sun, this . . . this person . . . was midnight. Her eyes were black and large, as if the pupils had expanded to consume all the iris. She had extravagant lashes and black hair, but it was her lips that drew my fascinated gaze. They were green. Not tinged with green, not a sickly green, but a flamboyant, defiant green. The green of jade. They matched a pendant around her neck that was an ornate object of jade and onyx, green and black, suggesting a face, a lewd, leering face.

There were other touches of green and black—earrings, a snake-pattern bracelet around her left wrist, fasteners down the front of her boots. And a ring on her left hand whose intricate design I could not make out.

Had Kayla seen this creature striding down the halls of her school, she would have curled into a little ball. For while Kayla was beautiful, and I liked to believe that I was at least pretty, this female creature had the beauty of cold, distant stars and silvery moonlight.

She was hypnotizing. Merely by existing, she redefined my ideas of beauty, for this was not mere physical perfection, this was seduction; this was the primordial, essential, eternal avatar of female sensuality walking nonchalantly down the empty hallway of a suburban high school.

She made me feel shrunken and small and ugly.

Her name was . . .

"Oriax," Messenger said.

4

"Messenger," Oriax said. She spoke with a voice full of silk, secrets, and slithering snakes. Like Messenger's, her voice was too near, too intimate, but it thrilled me. I whimpered. I couldn't help it. I had forgotten my panic, forgotten for the moment that I should not be in this place at all, that I had lost my memory, that I feared I was dead. All of that was submerged the moment I saw her. I wanted to worship her. I wanted to listen to any word that she cared to speak. I wanted to be her, to be a tiny *fraction* of her.

Oriax.

"Well, hello there . . ." she said to me, and then after a longish pause added, "you."

I grunted. Like a farm animal. I could not make a more complex sound.

"She's not bad-looking, really, eh, Messenger?

Daniel has done well for you. He must be feeling sorry for you, poor, pining, lovelorn Messenger."

Part of me was hearing her words, but a larger part of me was asking why Messenger hadn't already thrown himself at her feet. Messenger was a beautiful boy, but this . . . Oriax . . .

"Let her go, Oriax."

Oriax winked at me. "He wants me to let you go." She moved close to me, so close I could feel the heat of her body, so close I could smell a perfume that . . . and then, she walked around behind me and I was paralyzed with something that was both fear and desperate, unfamiliar desire.

I felt her hair brush the nape of my neck. I felt her breath on my skin. Her lips brushed the side of my neck, and my eyes rolled up in my head, and the blood left my limbs and my knees gave way.

"Susceptible little thing, isn't she?" Oriax said.

Messenger caught me as I fell. He put a hand under my back, and another hand reached for my shoulder but missed and instead slid over the fabric of my shirt to touch my arm.

For only a moment his skin and mine made contact.

And then I knew why I was not to touch Messenger, for in the few seconds of contact, flesh to flesh, I was assaulted by images I can barely bring myself to describe, for to describe them is to make the horrible real.

First, I saw a boy, maybe fifteen years old, stabbed though the belly with a sword.

Then a girl, perhaps fourteen, being lowered on the end of a chain, screaming, into a vat of foul, seething liquid.

A boy, a big kid who looked older than he probably was, with both hands and both feet gone, trying to run on stumps from a pack of wild dogs.

There were other images, less lurid, but I couldn't begin to comprehend them while dealing with these visions of helplessness and agony and utter, shrieking terror.

I cried out in pain and staggered back. Oriax threw

back her head and laughed with malicious delight, and I clutched my head as though to squeeze the memories out of my brain.

These were awful violations of human bodies and minds. Such pain. Such terrible sadness and loneliness.

"What *are* you?" I asked Messenger, my voice ragged.

"I thought he was a dream," Oriax taunted me.

I gritted my teeth. Tears had started, blurring my vision, glistening, foolish emblems of my weakness. "I don't have dreams like that. Those things . . . *Those things are not in my head!*"

Messenger looked solemn, but I thought I saw some hurt there as well. He had revealed something and was hurt by my violent reaction. He looked at me, and I could not match his gaze and lowered my eyes.

"Someday you will see the darkness inside yourself, Mara," he said in that too-near whisper of his.

"Oh, look, you've hurt Messenger's feelings," Oriax said. "Shall I comfort you, Messenger?" She moved closer to him. "Shall I, Messenger, my pretty boy?"

"Get away from me," he said.

And without seeming to move, she was six feet away, laughing and sticking out her tongue. "He's no fun, our Messenger," Oriax said to me. "You'll see. You'll want him, but you won't have him. You'll crave him desperately, oh yes, you will."

"He's a demon!" I said, practically spitting the word, as the images of our brief contact still churned vilely in my memory. That word, *demon*, wasn't in my thoughts until it came out of my mouth and I realized it was true. Or realized at least that I believed it.

"A demon?" Oriax repeated, disbelieving. "Our Messenger a demon? Don't be ridiculous. No, no, no. He's not a demon. I know a few demons, well, what you might call demons, and sadly our Messenger of Fear is no demon, unless demons mourn for their lost Ariadne."

"Leave us, Oriax. You've had your fun."

"Mmm, not yet, I haven't," she said. "But eventually."

She was gone, and I was filled with fear and a deep

disturbance that seemed to have a physical effect: I was trembling. Trembling all over, in every part of my body, from my knees to my heart to the muscles of my face, as though each individual cell was shaking.

"I am sorry I touched you, Mara," Messenger said. "It would have been kinder to let you fall."

I felt deeply unsettled. The vivid memories of that touch had begun to fade and I was glad of it. The memory of Oriax, too, seemed to lose some of its sharp detail, and for that I was sorry because I had never seen or imagined anyone quite like her. I wanted to hold that image in my mind until I had come to grips with it and decided just how . . .

Let her go, Oriax.

What did Messenger mean by that? How had she "had" me that she needed to let me go?

I recalled a sense of being released, and of that release filling me, however briefly, with a sense of loss but also a sense of relief. I had fallen when she released me, but she had never laid a finger on me.

Too much. Too much now crowded my brain. Too many feelings, too many wild emotions, too much fear, and . . . and something that was like fear but also held within it seeds of pleasure. I found that part of me wanted Oriax to come back. Even more of me wanted Messenger to speak to me, to explain, but also just to speak.

You'll crave him desperately, oh yes, you will.

No, that at least would never be true. I had burned myself on that hot stove and did not need a second reminder that Messenger was not to be touched.

But did I still want him to explain? Did I want him to reveal? Yes.

"Why is my memory all fuzzy?" I asked him.

He considered me for a moment and reached some kind of decision. He drew a deep breath, and this simple biological act lessened my fear somewhat, for I had begun to believe my own blurted remark—that he was a demon, or if not a demon, then some other nameless supernatural horror.

51

Did demons breathe in that particularly weary way? Did sadness and loss reveal themselves in demons' eyes?

I was confused. My feelings were all astray, rifled and tossed like a room that's been burglarized. My memory, my emotions, all of it was too much, but I had already fainted once and would not allow myself to do so again. Whatever else this was, it was a test of my strength, my will. I would not be weak.

"Your memory has been disturbed by the transition."

"Well, I need my memory."

"Do you?" He tilted his head and looked at me as if my image was evoking something from another time and place. He wasn't looking at me, Mara; he was looking at something I reminded him of.

"Look, Messenger," I said, trying to sound determined, "I don't know what you want of me, but I won't cooperate unless I know who I am and . . ." I hesitated there, for the next words would perhaps reveal too much of the vulnerability I felt. Then, with a sigh that fluttered in my chest, I finished, ". . . and *what* I am."

I swear that then he almost smiled. It was nothing that I could see, but the slight lessening in the rigidity of his features allowed me to think that he was possibly smiling.

"Yes. Memory," he said.

And then, I remembered.

5

I saw what I looked like. I saw my face. My body. And with it, memories of earlier stages of my life. Me a year ago. Me three years ago. Me as a little girl taking gymnastics.

My locker combination was 13-36-9.

My grade point average was 4.0.

I was five feet, five inches tall and hoped against all odds to grow taller.

I weighed 121 pounds.

I knew my social security number.

I knew my student ID number.

I knew my driver's license number, which surprised me because I didn't think I'd ever memorized that.

It was as if every number I'd ever known was coming bubbling up into my brain. My home was at number 72. My birthday was July 26. My phone number . . .

"That's not what matters," I said.

"I thought you wanted to see your memories," Messenger said.

"Those aren't the memories. Those aren't what I need. Did you do that to me? Can you turn my memory on and off?"

He surprised me by giving a direct answer. "Yes."

"That's not fair!" The words were out of my mouth before I'd even begun to think about them.

"Fair." He said the word with something like reverence. Like the word had deep significance to him. "I'm sorry you find me unfair, but I think you are mistaken. You don't yet understand, and whether it is fair or not in your judgment, I will hold your memories. I will hold them back."

"What? Who says? I mean, what?"

"It's part of the deal you made," Messenger said.

I froze.

"What?"

He did not repeat himself. So I did.

"What? What do you mean, it's the deal I made?"

"You must trust me, Mara."

"Trust you? I don't even know your name. I don't even know what you are. I don't know where we are or why. Trust you?"

"Yes, Mara. You must trust me."

I stared at him, and this time I did not lower my eyes but met his gaze. "What is this about?" I asked.

He could have easily sidestepped such a poorly phrased question. But he did not. Instead he chose to answer, emphasis always on "chose" because though I didn't yet know it, I was entirely in his power. At that moment, and for a long while after as well, I belonged to Messenger. I was his to control.

"This," he said without the least drama or emphasis, "is about true and false. Right and wrong. Good and evil. And justice, Mara. This is about justice. And balance. And . . ." He nodded as if to himself rather than to me. ". . . and redemption."

I said nothing. What is there to be said after such a speech?

He seemed vaguely amused that he had silenced me. And he took the opportunity to point a finger and invite my gaze to turn in the direction he indicated.

"It is also, at this moment, about Samantha Early."

And there she was, Samantha Early, no longer at school but at her laptop computer in a Starbucks. She was chewing on her upper lip, concentrating, typing in stops and starts. Pause, then a sudden flurry. Pause, then a sudden flurry.

"What is she writing?" I asked.

"She'd already written it when she died," Messenger said. "As to what she wrote, go and look."

We were outside the Starbucks, looking in through the window. I went for the door, reached for it with my hand, and found that it seemed to slip away. I thought at first I had just missed, but a second attempt had the same result. On a third attempt I watched carefully and moved my hand slowly. I expected to see my hand pass in a ghostly way through the solid object. And what does it reveal about my state of mind that I expected that?

But rather than my insubstantial hand passing through a solid object, it was the door handle that moved. It was there, and then, an instant before my fingers would have touched it, it was gone. And the moment I withdrew my hand, it was back.

"You cannot alter what you see around you," Messenger instructed. "You may see all but touch nothing. What you see is all past, and the past may not be changed."

"How do I see what she's writing if I can't open the stupid door?" I said. I was annoyed by the door, irrationally annoyed. It was strange to be irritated by something so small in these wanderings with a strange boy through an impossible universe. But maybe it was easier or safer to be bothered by things that seemed familiar.

The deal I made.

Did I even want to know how I had come to make a deal with Messenger? And why had he said that I may see but not touch? Why *may* and not *can*? That word

MICHAEL GRANT

choice hinted at rules, and rules come from a person or institution.

"I need time," I said. "I need to . . . to rest." If I could just sit down somewhere, digest, put things together. Think.

"It's a lot to understand," Messenger allowed. "But the understanding will only come by living it."

"Or you could explain it," I snapped.

"Do you want to know what Samantha Early is writing?"

I have a fatal weakness: I am the cat curiosity killed. "Yes, of course I want to know. The girl is going to kill herself. Maybe her writing will tell us why."

"Then see," Messenger said.

It was a challenge. Or a test. He wanted to know whether I could find a way into the coffee shop.

The thing I "may" not do was to alter anything around me. I could not touch, could not change. I had a thought then and wondered if it made sense. I could ask Messenger, but I sensed that this would disappoint him, and absurdly, I did not want to disappoint him.

We had become teacher and student, and I have always been a good, if not perfect, student. It's one of the things I dislike about myself, that willingness to please. Sometimes I dislike it so much that I pick fights with people just to show that I will not be their slave. But this was not the time, and Messenger was not the person. He held my memories. He had power over me. If I were ever to get back to my own reality, escape this . . . this whatever it was . . . then it would be through Messenger.

It occurred to me then that I had a project due. My science project, which was . . . I couldn't recall what it was, but that single fugitive thought, that anxiety, had crept through whatever blocked my memory and reminded me that I did truly have a need to get back.

My God, was that really my only reason for needing to get back to my life?

I took a deep breath and walked straight toward the Starbucks' brick-and-plate-glass storefront. I steeled myself for impact and closed my eyes in a flinch.

There was no impact. I was on the other side of the window, inside the coffee shop, standing behind Samantha Early as she typed and paused and typed some more.

This is what I saw on her monitor:

what the French call "l'esprit de l'escalier". It means "the spirit of the staircase", but what it's really about is the way you always think of the perfect comeback after it's too late, after you're on the bus heading home from school, or in your mom's car, or on the staircase, and then, ah hah! The perfect comeback.

Now Jessica knew what she should have said to Elise. She should have said, "I am sad for you that you care so much about how I look and what I wear. It must be hard for you being so superficial."

That's what she should have said. But instead she

Messenger was beside me. I did not turn to look at

him but said, "She's a pretty good writer. I wonder what the story is about."

"Wonder," he said. It wasn't an echo, it was an instruction.

So I wondered, and gasped as the whole of it, the 72 pages that preceded that single screen, and the 241 pages that would come after it, were all suddenly known to me. As if I had read it all. No, not that, because even when you read a book, you forget a lot of it. This book, *The Nightmare Clique*, was known to me in every detail.

"It's about a group of high school girls who use supernatural powers to bully kids they don't like," I said.

"That's the story. Is it the real purpose of the book?"

I shook my head. "No. No, it's really about Samantha. She is Jessica. And the nightmare clique is Kayla and her friends."

Messenger nodded. "Shall we look at the happiest day in Samantha's life?"

I was not so naive that I didn't realize there was a danger in this. Seeing Samantha happy would only emphasize the awful tragedy of her death. But Messenger didn't wait for an answer. Without any sense of movement we were suddenly in a different place. We were at Yolo's, and Samantha was loading a large Styrofoam dish of frozen yogurt with Reese's Pieces and Butterfinger crumbles. She paid at the register and glanced around, nervous that someone from school would see her piling on calories.

As soon as she sat down, she ate a big spoonful and while she crunched the cold candies, she checked her email on her phone. I saw the email, and in some way I could not yet hope to explain, I saw it more fully in Samantha's mind.

It was from a literary agent.

I am very pleased to tell you that I would love to represent The Nightmare Clique. *I think there is an excellent chance of selling it to a major publisher, and if you will sign the attached document, I will get to work immediately.*

"She thinks she's going to publish it!" I said. I was excited. There have been times when I thought of becoming a writer, but I would never have had the courage to actually submit a manuscript at my age. Samantha and I were the same age, and she had been brave enough to risk rejection.

I had pitied her. Now I admired her.

"Twenty-seven days on from this moment, HarperCollins will agree to publish Samantha's book," Messenger said. "Samantha will read that letter seven times, will have no choice but to read it seven times. She will be frustrated by her compulsion, but she will also be elated. She will tell herself that now, at last, everything will change for the better."

"But that's not the way it works out," I said.

"No," Messenger said, and we were back in Samantha's room, and her body was on the floor of her bedroom, stiffening, growing cold as it awaited her mother's horrifying discovery that her only child was gone.

I shook my head. "I can't do this, okay? I can't. You have to let me go. I don't want to see this. I don't want to feel this, Messenger, whoever you are, *what*ever you are, I don't . . ." I was crying. It should have been humiliating, crying in front of him.

"No one prefers this path," he said. His voice was flat and devoid of emotion. But I saw something like nausea reflected in his expression. "No one would choose to feel another's pain. But this is my . . . This is *your* fate, Mara."

"No," I said sharply. "This is all some kind of creepy trick!"

He didn't deign to reply to that. He waited, silent, as the truth, or at least a part of it, began to sink in.

"I'm being punished," I said.

Again, he said nothing. I wondered if I could find a way to feel what he was feeling—to know his mind as I had so easily penetrated the mind of Samantha Early—but when I turned my thoughts that way, I felt his mind retreat and fend me off.

It was like the door handle. I could see him, but I was not allowed to touch him. Not physically, not mentally. I was an open book to him, and he was closed to me.

I am not to be touched.

"Not all my . . . *our* . . . duties are quite so grim," he said at last. "This terrible matter will hold for a while. And I think you could do with a change of scenery."

6

The change of scenery was sudden and extreme. One moment we were standing over Samantha Early's body, and the next we were in the back seat of a car. The transfer was carried out by no usual earthly means and this was attested to by the fact that I never felt even the slightest acceleration, though we had gone in a flash from stationary to sixty-four miles an hour.

A boy and a girl were in the front seat. The girl was driving. The boy was clowning, doing a duck-face rendition of a Rihanna song. The girl laughed.

"What is this?" I asked in a whisper. It was a natural human instinct to whisper, though I had slowly begun to realize that nothing I did would be seen, and nothing I said would be heard by the people we watched.

"This is Emma and Liam," Messenger said.

Liam was a ginger, so Irish-looking he could have

been the poster boy for an Irish tourism ad campaign. Emma was very nearly his opposite. She was Latina, with extraordinarily voluminous brown hair, dark eyes, and smooth skin that I admired.

"Is that the place?" Liam asked as they drove past a narrow, rutted driveway marked by a mailbox that had not seen a delivery in a very long time. He was rubbing Emma's neck and she was enjoying it.

You can sense when a couple is a couple, when they are so close that silence is as good as talking, and when talking is a series of sentences left dangling because you know the other person knows what you mean. A couple is close when most of what passes between them is tacit, unvoiced, not for display, not for signaling to outsiders. I had the vague feeling that perhaps my parents had been like that once. I had the definite feeling that I had never known that kind of relationship.

"Yep. Missed it." The road was two-lane, trees on both sides, arching overhead, blocking the rapidly failing light of a cold sun. Emma pulled the car into a

U-turn and winced when she heard the bumper scrape over branches. "I cannot have a mark on the car. You know my dad."

"Sadly, yes, I do know your dad."

"He's actually—"

"A good guy. Yeah, Emma, I know. Someday I'll be a father with a daughter and—"

"You'll be just like him."

"Well, much hotter, of course."

"Don't say the word 'hot' anywhere near the words 'your dad,'" Emma said.

"The word 'hot' is all about me," Liam said. "And you."

"There's the road."

They drove back to the missed pull-off, then at walking speed followed the overgrown path until it reached a clearing. In the clearing was a barn with a collapsed roof, and a tiny house that must once have been loved. The sagging porch had long ago been painted in bright colors, and someone had carved gingerbread appliqué to give the place a quaint, almost fairy-tale look.

"You sure no one's here?" Liam asked, looking dubious.

"It belongs to my grandmother," Emma said, and drove the car around the back so that even if someone did happen down the road, it would not be seen.

"The grandmother—"

"Yes, the one in the nursing home. Granny Batista. She hasn't been here in, like, a year, and I've been watering her plants."

"I'm going to water *your* plants."

"Really, Liam? That's your sexual innuendo? Water my plants?"

They both laughed, Liam as much as Emma, taking pleasure in the silliness of the exchange.

They climbed out and Liam came around to the driver's side and leaned Emma back against the car. They kissed, and this went on for quite a while and was clearly becoming a prelude to more.

Messenger watched impassively, but I was feeling most uncomfortable. "Do we have to be Peeping Toms?"

"We can move forward."

Suddenly, the two young lovers began to move faster, faster, a video on fast-forward. They kissed, broke apart, moved like manic robots to the door of the house, through the door.

Messenger stood waiting. He glanced around at the trees. "Dogwood and hemlock," he said as though answering a question. "Oak as well, of course."

"Hemlock. Isn't that poisonous?" Seriously, this he would discuss with me? Botany?

"It can be. It's a favorite of witches."

I played that back in my head, wondering if there had been irony surrounding the word "witches". I heard no hint of humor. And suddenly we were in a hallway in the house, outside a closed and locked door.

We didn't wait long before Emma and Liam came out, somewhat less fully dressed than they had been, but decent, arms around each other.

"There are chips and cookies downstairs," Emma said. "You need to keep your strength up."

That earned a laugh and they rushed downstairs to feed. By the time they reached the kitchen, Messenger and I were waiting for them.

"Remind me to check the car for scratches or anything. The mileage will look like I went to the Walgreens, but if it's scraped up or has crushed green leaves or whatever . . ."

"Your dad," Liam said.

"He's just . . . you know, old. I mean, your mom and dad are what, thirty-two?"

"Thirty-three and thirty-four," Liam said, ripping open a bag of chips.

"And my dad is sixty," Emma said. "Sixty and raised in a little mountain village in Nowhere, Guatemala. He thinks different."

"He hates love," Liam joked.

"No, he just hates sex if it involves his daughter."

"We're always careful. I mean, all rubbered up, sir!" He snapped a salute.

"Oh, good, you can tell my dad that. Tell him it's okay because you were wearing protection. Just be ready to outrun a bullet."

Liam fed her a chip. She tried to crunch it in some sensual, provocative way, but most of the chip broke off and hit the floor. They both laughed and Liam gathered her to him.

"I love you," he said.

"I love you, too."

"No," Liam insisted, his voice heavy with emotion. "I don't mean like a throwaway line. I mean that I think about you every hour of every day. I see you every time I close my eyes. I don't shower after we've been together because I want to be able to smell you on my skin." He hesitated, feeling embarrassed as his fair skin colored. "That last might have been a little creepy."

"Not even a little creepy," she said, her own voice husky. "And I love you that same way. Desperate love.

You know? Like sometimes it just kind of wells up, and for a few seconds I can't breathe or swallow."

Suddenly angry, Liam spun away from Emma. "We have to get past this. We have to be together. I mean, what is the problem? Why can't I just go to your dad and say, 'Look, Mr. Aguilar, Emma and I love each other, and I know you still think about me breaking that trellis when I was twelve, but let it go, all right? Let it go.'"

"Mmmm. That will so not work."

"Let me try at least."

She held him out at arm's length. "Liam, listen to me: it won't work. He'll ground me for three months. There will be no way for us to see each other. To be together. Like this."

Liam cursed. Not at Emma—at life, it seemed. He tore into the bag of cookies with enough violence to cause half of them to scatter across the countertop. They ate in silence, glum, chewing and drinking juice.

"Please tell me this doesn't end like Samantha Early," I said.

Messenger did not answer. He was watching them. Having tastefully not intruded on their lovemaking, he watched now with a palpable hunger. He swallowed and I saw that even as he watched them he was seeing another image, a faraway image.

"I have to water the plants," Emma said.

"Yep."

And just like that, we were in the back seat of the car again, and Emma was driving as Liam distracted her with light kisses on the side of her neck.

"What do you think of them?" Messenger asked.

"What do you mean?"

"Your opinion. Your judgment. That is our subject now, the question of your instincts."

I shifted uncomfortably. I did not like the idea of being judged, certainly not of being judged on my ability to judge others. But Messenger waited, knowing, I suppose, that I would answer, whatever my qualms.

"I like them. They're in love," I said.

"Are they? Did you look inside them?"

"What? You mean, poke inside their heads? No. Of course not."

"Then how do you know whether this is love or mere lust?" He seemed honestly perplexed.

"It's pretty obvious."

"Is it?" He sighed. "I suppose it is for you. I must resort to less delicate means. I have filled myself with their memories and feel what they feel. Yes. It is love."

"Duh." I whispered the word. I don't know if Messenger heard me or not.

Night had fallen, turning the forest around us into a place of eldritch fears, a fairy-tale forest wherein might lurk witches with interests in gingerbread and plump, flavorful children. The headlights cast irregular circles of light on the road but did not reach beyond the ditch to our right or the tangle of weeds to our left.

"And what do you think of that? Of love?" Messenger asked me.

"Okay, that's getting—"

Suddenly his insinuating voice, that whisper that

always seemed to be directly into my ear, became strident. "Understand something, Mara: you will answer my questions. You will reveal everything to me and hold nothing back."

It was said with undeniable authority. His tone was not pleading, nor was it cruel. He stated it as a simple fact, as though it was beyond question. And as he spoke, he seemed to grow, to become a foot taller and as much wider, and a cold, dark light shone from him.

Then he returned to his normal size, although how could I know what was normal for this creature?

"Understand that I ask you questions out of respect. In the hope that you will understand that you must . . . that you *may* . . . trust me. I can as easily enter your mind as the minds of any of those we meet. But if you are open and honest with me, Mara, I will not do that."

I was feeling that I'd been pushed around just about enough. And I was readying a devastating response when—

"Look out!"

At the same instant the car swerved sharply and there was the sound of impact. Stiff rubber and unyielding steel on flesh.

And a frantic squealing sound that went on and on, rising, falling, a visceral cry that spoke wordlessly of pain.

Emma pulled the car to the side, almost into the ditch, and jumped out, followed immediately by Liam.

The squeal came from an ancient dog, gray in the muzzle, with shaggy tan fur. The dog, a mix of who knew how many breeds, dragged itself sideways, trailing blood, to the side of the road and lay there, panting, unable to go farther.

"Oh, God!" I gasped. The dog's side was ruptured. Its fur became ever more matted as blood seeped out.

"We have to get it to a vet!" Liam cried as he dropped down beside the dog. "Oh, we're so sorry, boy, we are so sorry." He stroked a clean patch of dry fur behind the dog's left ear.

"We can't!" Emma cried. "My dad!"

"This dog is messed up; we can't leave him here like this," Liam argued, but already I could see the way he blinked, doubting his own certainty.

The dog mewled. It was not urgent. It was not a plea for help. It was sad and accepting. The dog neither knew that it was dying nor that it might yet be saved. It only knew pain and that its legs would no longer raise it up off the pavement. Its tail moved once, twice.

"We have to get out of here," Emma fretted. She went around to the front of the car and moaned upon seeing a dent, a bloody dent, in the right front bumper. "Oh, my God, oh, my God. I have to clean off the blood and get home right now!"

She was close to panic, and Liam left the whimpering dog's side reluctantly and went to comfort her.

"Someone's going to come by and see us here," Liam said, glancing nervously down the road. "If they do, they might pull over to help. Then we're out of luck. But we can't leave him suffering like this."

"We could drop him off somewhere and drive off."

"Carry a bloody dog in the car? What if we get pulled over? What if the car breaks down? What if there's a security camera at the vet? We have to . . . to put him out of his misery."

"Maybe if we left him, someone else would come along." Then she surrendered. Her shoulders sagged and she shook her head, not in denial but in rejection of her own desperate plans.

The dog made another soft mewling sound, then a yip of pain.

They stared at each other until Emma said, "I can't do it. I know we have to, but I can't. I can't."

"Make up your mind," Liam snapped, then apologized. "I'm sorry. I—"

"It's—" Emma said, and waved a hand, as though that movement could push terrible choices away.

"I'll do it," Liam said. "I'll drive. I can do this. I can do this."

They got back in the car, with Liam behind the

wheel. He threw the car into reverse and backed down the road a hundred feet.

"Did he stop moving? Maybe he's dead," Emma said, biting her fingernails. Tears were flowing freely.

"I'm sorry, boy. I'm so sorry," Liam said. Then he put the transmission into drive, sent the car rolling forward.

There was an agonizing bump as the right front wheel went over the dog. And a second bump as the rear wheel finished the job.

The car sped away.

Messenger and I watched their tail-lights glow in the dark. And then, we were back in the car. Emma and Liam were crying and cursing and apologizing still to the dog or to the heavenly powers or perhaps to themselves. Both were shaken and weeping.

Messenger said, "What is your judgment, Mara?"

"My judgment? What are you talking about? It's sad, that's my judgment."

The car stopped moving. Emma and Liam stopped

moving. Outside the wind still ruffled dark oak trees and sinister hemlock, but within the car only Messenger and I could move.

"They've done wrong," Messenger said. "They've listened to the worst in themselves and acted in ways that upset the balance of Isthil, the balance of justice and wickedness. The crime demands a price be paid. So, I ask again, Mara. What is your judgment?"

7

"I don't know what—" I fell silent because I saw someone approaching the car, walking down the road toward us. It was a young man, maybe twenty years old, not much older. He wore a white hoodie and blue jeans.

Messenger spotted him, drew what seemed to my ears to be a nervous breath, and sat back in the seat. He rolled down the window.

The man in the hoodie ambled up, loose-limbed, thin, and not very tall, but with that easy sense of command that spoke of great confidence and an absence of fear.

"Daniel," Messenger said.

"Messenger. Mara." Daniel leaned over, resting his forearms on the roof of the car but lowering his head enough to make eye contact with Messenger. From where I sat, I could see only the lower part of Daniel's face.

I was consumed by curiosity, wanting to ask

MICHAEL GRANT

Messenger just what he meant by Isthil. Had I even heard that correctly? But this new arrival—not to mention Messenger's eternal taciturnity—made follow-up questions impossible.

Daniel's voice was like Messenger's in that it seemed as if he, too, was whispering in my ear. But Messenger was serious and soft-spoken, while Daniel's voice carried a hint that he might just possess a sense of humor.

"Have you dealt with the Early matter yet?" Daniel asked.

"We have begun," Messenger said.

"Ah, so you're being nonlinear," Daniel said. "I remember a time when you were a prisoner of Flatworld, Messenger." That was perhaps some sort of joke, I wasn't sure, and I didn't understand it.

Daniel's voice grew more professional. The pleasantries were over. "Where is she in her progress?" The "she" was clearly me. Daniel indicated me with an outthrust chin.

"She's calmed," Messenger said.

"Memory?"

"I don't want to overload her."

"Ah," Daniel said. He dropped to a squat, which let him look me in the eye. "So you have no real idea what's going on. No idea why you're here."

I shook my head.

"And you are frightened, nervous, but also excited, I see." He frowned and tilted his head sideways. "You are Messenger's student, not mine, but I will tell you by way of reassurance that it will all become clear to you. In time."

Messenger stiffened a bit at this reassurance. I think he wanted me uncertain.

"We had a visit," Messenger said significantly.

"Oh?"

"Oriax," Messenger said.

The two of them exchanged hard looks at that. I would have expected a leer, a wink, a raised eyebrow, but there was none of that. No sense that they were referring to what had to be the most beautiful young woman either of them had ever or would ever encounter.

"That's very quick," Daniel said. "Very quick. Who do you think she's after?"

"She came to us while we were on the Samantha Early matter."

"Oriax is not known for her directness," Daniel said. "So it's most likely something else. Someone else. Though, of course, she could be counting on us believing that."

"Can I ask a question?" I said. My voice sounded squeaky in my own ears.

Messenger turned to look at me, and Daniel's face went blank. He pulled back, making it clear that I was to speak only to Messenger.

"You will have a great many questions," Messenger said coldly. "But you will learn by observing. Later you will learn by doing. At this moment you will learn by remaining silent."

If I expected to find some sympathy from Daniel, I was mistaken. Messenger had shot me down, and Daniel had merely waited for it to be over.

But I was tired of being frightened and kept in the dark. I was going to ask my question. And later, when I had other questions, I would ask those, too.

"What is Oriax?" I asked.

The question surprised Messenger. One eyebrow rose fractionally. "Not who? You ask 'what'?"

"She's not human," I said, surprising myself with my certainty. It had only just then come to me. The way they spoke of Oriax revealed, if not fear from the two males, at least wariness. They saw something in her that I had not, which meant they knew more than I, and what they knew was that Oriax was not merely a beautiful woman with unusually small feet.

"She's quick," Daniel said to Messenger.

"Yes," Messenger admitted. Coming from him, it did not sound like a compliment. "The time will come when you understand Oriax and her kind. That day will be terrible for you, and worse for someone else."

Daniel was gone. No poof, no flash of light, no explosion, just, suddenly, gone. And the car was moving again. Liam and Emma were crying again and talking about the "poor doggie".

"We love each other, why is that so damn hard?" Liam moaned. "Why can't we just be together?"

"Wait, is this the right way?" Emma looked around, turned to look back, looked right through me, right through me as if I was not there.

And I understood her concern, for a mist was creeping over the road. It was the color of yellowed teeth. It was the same mist that had seemed to creep across my body. It moved at a pace that was all out of sync with the rushing speed of the car. The mist was leisurely but relentless. And as it caressed the vehicle, it was not parted or blown aside by the passage of that now frail-seeming machine.

The car was running; I could hear the engine, I could hear and feel the vibration of tires on pavement. But there could be no sense of speed because the mist blocked all evidence of passing landscape.

Finally Liam took his foot off the gas pedal and the

car grew quieter, rolling now rather than being propelled. Slower and slower, tires making a hollow sound.

Without warning, Messenger and I were no longer in the back seat but stood beneath a blasted mockery of a tree, a tree that looked as if it had never borne a leaf.

The mist did not touch us but surrounded us at a distance, hemming us in, leaving a gloomy, unreal space no more than fifty feet across. The mist was also above us, blocking any hint of sky. I felt the tickling of panic. Somehow amidst all the evidence of overturned laws of physics, all the unnatural flouting of the unseen but omnipresent laws that define our world, it was this, this creeping, sentient mist that most impressed upon my strained senses and raw emotions that I was in a place that was fundamentally at odds with reality. When the basic rules, up and down, fast and slow, before and now and after, were so casually suspended and upended, how was I ever to feel a moment's safety? Daniel had said I would understand, eventually. But why should I trust him any more than these proofs of the instability of space and time?

The car with Emma and Liam nosed into that strange and unnatural circle and came to rest.

The two teens stared. At us. At *us*.

"They see us," I said.

Liam tried to start the car again, but the engine would not catch. I could see them debating, worried, unsettled by this place and by the two people who now awaited them.

Finally Liam climbed out. He had a large flashlight, one of the black metal ones that police use both to shine a light and serve as a bludgeon. Liam held the light threateningly, as if contemplating that latter use.

"Who are you?" Liam demanded.

Emma stood at his side.

"Emma, I thought you were going to stay in the car! Get back in the car!" Liam cried.

"I . . . I don't think I got out," Emma said, her voice abashed, whispering but with her whispers magnified, bounced back at her by the mist.

She stood close to her lover, took his free arm in hers, forming a united front. They took strength from each other and together were stronger than either alone.

"Okay, who are you and what is going on?" Liam demanded, pushing his voice to a lower, more determined register.

"I am the Messenger."

"We're not looking for trouble," Emma said. "We just want to get out of here."

"That will not be possible," Messenger said. "Yet."

Liam pushed away from Emma, preparing himself for a fight. I liked the way he looked. He was scared but resolute. He was determined to protect Emma. And she was just as prepared to defend him. Someone had once said to me that the thing to understand about love was that you were two people who had each other's back. That you were two against the world. Someone had said that. But who? The memory had just been there, it had just appeared, as if my memory were my own to command, but when I searched for detail, I was frustrated. It was almost as if some counterpart to the mist was inside me, in my mind, defining what I could know and what I could not.

But then that mental mist retreated—oh so grudgingly—showing me just a little more.

I gasped, for I could see him now. My father. I could see him in memory, and with that single picture, that yellowed photograph, came other facts.

He's white, my father. It's my mother who gave me my Chinese physiognomy. I took very little of my looks from his genes, but I took on more of his personality. He's a soldier, my father, a professional soldier. United States Army. A captain. A stocky man with wide shoulders and hair turned gray too early. A serious man.

And he's dead.

The realization opened in my memory like some dark flower that greeted not sunlight but the blackness of night.

They had handed the folded flag to me. The officer in charge of the burial had been solemn and correct, compassionate but distant, and I had thought, even then, even as a child of nine, that the officer must do this a lot. How many times had he walked the folded, dark-blue-and-white triangle of flag to a wife or a husband or a child?

I was drawn out of my sad reverie by what Messenger was saying. It was a phrase I would hear again. "You have done wrong. You must first acknowledge the wrong, and then you must atone."

"What?" Emma demanded. "What do you mean, *atone*?"

"Do you acknowledge the wrong you have done?"

"The dog?" Liam said. "We didn't mean to do that—that was an accident."

I wanted to jump in and point out that hitting the dog the first time was an accident; running over it again was just to cover up the fact that they had been together. But I had begun to feel that I was watching something of great importance. I wanted to see what Messenger would do next, though as I thought about it more, I began to dread it. What if Messenger killed them?

But Messenger just stood and waited. Emma and Liam shifted uncomfortably and made a few halfhearted attempts to justify themselves. But it was clear that they, too, were fully aware that they had indeed done wrong.

Guilt is a parasite on the soul, a worm that begins small and grows, grows, feeding on every moment of fleeting happiness. It stabs at you when you laugh. It cuts when you recognize beauty, receive affection, experience joy. It reminds you at the very worst moments that you have done wrong and are not worthy of happiness.

I did not then ask myself how I had come by this knowledge. How should I know so well what shame and guilt can do? But at that moment I was still weak from the memory of my father, mourning, I suppose, for a man whose place in my mind had been reduced to a still photograph and a handful of dusty facts.

And, too, I was fascinated and repelled by the place and situation I found myself in. So I did not ask how I knew what guilt could do. I was like a doctor who, recognizing a disease, has forgotten medical school and his practice and retained only that barest dry and useless knowledge.

"Okay, we're sorry," Liam said finally. "Really. Okay? I panicked. You don't understand."

"My apprentice will understand," Messenger said, "and thus, so will I."

Liam and Emma both looked at me. It was only after they had stared expectantly for a few seconds that I realized Messenger was talking about me.

"Apprentice?" It came out squeaky, that single word. I almost laughed. I wanted to laugh. Because, after all, this was really just some kind of dream or hallucination or . . . or something.

What it was not, what it could not be, was me as Messenger's *apprentice*. The very idea was like a steel cage being erected around me, like I was watching the bars being put in place, confining, defining, controlling.

I felt like prisoners must feel facing the judge who pronounces their sentence.

"No," I said. I shook my head violently. "No," I said again.

Messenger's face wore a look I had suspected it might be capable of, but had not truly seen until this moment. His expression was one of compassion. He was not glorying in my fear; he pitied me. He understood what he had just told me. He understood what I was feeling. He could see the panic rising in me like the mercury in a boiling thermometer.

"No, no, no," I said.

And that's when I saw through the mist. The mist did not part—it did not cease encircling us—but it became less opaque, so that I saw a tableau. I saw two people. One was Messenger. The other was me.

And I heard my own voice distorted by wracking sobs of what I believe was remorse, though I had no memory of it. Sobbing. Holding myself with my arms across my chest. My head was bowed. My face was distorted by emotion present and emotion past. I had, I felt, been sad for a long time.

In this tableau Messenger never spoke—he just stood there before me, wearing the same expression of compassion he had revealed only moments before. I was the one speaking—though words so distorted by anguish would have been hard for a person unfamiliar with me to make out. But I could hear and understand them clearly. They were words that sealed my fate. Words that trapped me without hope of escape.

"Yes," I sobbed. "Yes, yes, I will. I will. I will do it. I have to do it. I will atone."

"If you choose this fate, you must speak these words: You will be my teacher."

My sobbing self spoke them. "You will be my teacher."

Messenger said, "I will be your student."

And my anguished self repeated them and wiped tears away. "I will be your student."

"And when I am judged ready, I will faithfully execute my office."

"And . . . and . . ." The me I saw, that living memory,

strained to recall the exact words. "I will . . . I mean, when I am judged ready, I will faithfully execute my office."

"I will *be* the Messenger of Fear."

The tableau faded from view. I looked at Messenger and it was as if he looked through me, saw all the way down into my soul and knew things about me that I refused to acknowledge but that he understood.

I looked at his coat with its skull buttons. I looked at the terrible ring, the distorted, screaming face. Most of all, I recalled the moment when I had touched him and had been flooded with images so unsettling, so disturbing, that even the pale memory freezes my blood. I guessed, or perhaps at some point in my forgotten past he had told me, but in any event I understood then, *understood* that there was no escape, that I had no choice in the matter, not any longer. My fate was settled.

And the words came from my own mouth now, not from the image from memory but still as if spoken in a dream.

"I will be the Messenger of Fear."

8

None of this last had been seen or heard by Liam and Emma. No time had elapsed for them since Messenger had said, "My apprentice will understand, and thus, so will I."

The two frightened kids waited for me as though I was to question them.

"My apprentice will lay her palm against your cheek, and if you do not resist, it will be quick and not unpleasant."

Would I? I supposed I must. But what I wanted to do was yell at Messenger to give me everything, not to just dole out bits and pieces of myself in whatever amount was necessary to manipulate me. To tell me everything, about himself, about this impossible reality, if reality it was.

I was trapped, yes, but that did not compel me to

be docile. Perhaps I was trapped, yes, but . . . but even a very good trap often has an escape route.

I was equivocating, beginning to feel my way toward escape, though a few minutes before I had been ready to accept my fate. There is something rebellious in me, something that does not readily accept limitation.

But then, I pondered the scene that had just been revealed to me by Messenger. I had been sobbing. That was me—me, Mara—and I had been sobbing with terrible remorse. What could possibly have happened to cause me to sob my heart out that way? What had happened?

What had I *done*?

Messenger, my teacher. Me, his student.

I will be the Messenger of Fear.

What did that mean?

One thing was clear as I drew a mental cloak over my defiant urges: right now it meant obeying him. Until I figured out what was happening.

Somehow, by some means I could not begin to

guess at, I was in a very different reality with rules that included being able to move effortlessly from place to place, to freeze time or speed it up. To simply know things that should be unknowable. To intrude on thoughts that were not my own. A place of sentient mists and stunning women and, above all, the boy in black, the Messenger with his mysterious manner and strange dress and too-intimate voice.

I had not forgotten—no, far from it—the visions I had seen on making physical contact with Messenger. I cautioned myself that however calm and controlled he seemed now, he was a creature whose mind was filled with dark scenes of unspeakable wickedness.

He was, in short, dangerous.

Time had passed since Messenger had warned Liam and Emma that I would be touching them, but if the two of them were impatient, they gave no sign. They waited, not frozen, but like a GIF, a loop, eyes blinking, mouths breathing, their fingers intertwined, the ginger boy and the dark girl.

Messenger waited too, and watched, interested by how I was digesting all this new information. It angered me, that calm way of his, that solemn but compassionate watching and waiting. The *patience* of him.

But what was I to do? This was his world, and I was sworn to be his student. Later I would find the way out, oh yes, as you see, already I was thinking of escape—even while suspecting that my thoughts were as open to him as the page of any book.

Flushing at that unsettling notion, I broke my trance and laid my hand against Liam's faintly freckled cheek and against Emma's at the same time, standing between the two of them, an intruder in their relationship. But that rude and too-familiar physical transgression was nothing compared to what I next experienced. For into my reeling mind poured the whole history of Emma and Liam.

I saw Liam's first memory. He was on his back, looking up, and into his field of vision came a woman. She seemed tired, her eyes dark, hair straggling, but she smiled like a madonna when she saw him.

His mother. I was seeing Liam as a baby, seeing his mother. I saw images of his father as well, a large man, with big hands and a look of perpetual skepticism. I saw his pets, his friends, his room, the posters on his wall as he grew older.

All of this came to me as a sort of accelerated slide show, pictures tumbling over pictures, snippets of video mingling with audio tracks, a vast hallucinogenic data dump.

A particular video caught my eye, and I plucked it out to examine. Liam was in a classroom and, judging by the other students around him, it must have been recent, from no more than a few months ago. In this, Liam was looking at Emma. I saw it as a glance, a look away to the whiteboard and the teacher, a glance back, a look away, a glance, until Emma happened to spy him looking at her and she met his gaze with an arched brow and a dubious expression.

At the same time I saw Emma's path to that same

moment. I saw her earliest memories, her mother and father, her brothers, her cat, her room.

I felt ashamed. I had become a stalker, an invader of minds, an intruder in memories I had no right to. And yet it was fascinating and exhilarating at almost a physical level, a rush, a thrill ride. A nauseating intrusion, but with my own memory reduced to a few pencil sketches, this trove of memories and sensations—for I could feel the emotion in each memory—was luxurious. I swam in the warm waters of memories that were not my own.

Finally, reluctantly, I broke contact.

There were tears on my cheeks.

"They love each other," I said. It was no great revelation, but I had felt the intensity of that emotion and knew it in a way that left me feeling small and unimportant. Love, yes, the love I no doubt felt for my parents and a half-remembered brother, but this was a different thing. This was not a long-burning candle; it was roaring fire. This was desire and need and a willing surrender that empowered.

"Yes," Messenger agreed. "And what of the wrong they have done?"

I frowned, not sure quite what he meant, though I had as well felt Liam and Emma's panic and self-loathing at the violent act they had committed.

"They're good people," I said.

"Yes," Messenger agreed. "What of the wrong they have done?"

"I . . . I don't know what you want from me."

"I want to know your thoughts, Mara. What of the wrong they have done?"

"Can't you just open my head up and see for yourself?" I snapped. "If I can do it, you can. You have, obviously. You're the one keeping me from seeing my own memories." I was becoming agitated, sickened by the terrible violation I had committed in stealing the memories of these two decent kids, kids my own age, not monsters, just kids who had made a very bad mistake.

And yet . . . and yet did I not want to see still more?

Did I not still wish that I was myself experiencing their intensity of feeling? There was a hunger in me that might be fed by gorging on borrowed emotion.

Messenger said, "I *can* do many things, Mara. But you will learn nothing from my reading of your mind. To learn you must form your thoughts and emotions into expression. What. Of. The. *Wrong?*"

I threw up my hands, helpless. I looked pleadingly at Liam and Emma—my God, I knew them each better than I knew myself—as if they could somehow save me from my own guilt. But, of course, neither of them understood that I had just dined on their most intimate experiences.

"I guess," I said, "they should . . . pay something. Be made to . . . They should . . ."

I could go no further. Messenger relented then and turned away from me to face the two frightened kids. "This wrong demands punishment," he said. "I offer you a game. If you win, you will go free, unbothered by me or by my apprentice."

"A game?" Liam echoed in obvious confusion.

"A game," Messenger said. "If you win, you go free. If you lose, then you will face the thing you fear most."

"What . . . what game?" Emma asked, with a nervous glance at Liam. "What's the game?"

"We will consider," Messenger said.

"Wait," Liam protested. "We're just supposed to sit here and wait, not knowing? I mean, what the hell, man?"

Emma was ready to jump in and also demand some kind of resolution, but whatever she had to say, I didn't hear it then, for we were no longer with Emma and Liam. We were once again with Samantha Early.

9

It was a school lunchroom. Noisy, chaotic, smelling of grease and overcooked Brussels sprouts. On the walls were posters exhorting the team to beat the Redwood Giants. There was a nutrition poster on the wall next to the food line. The tables were round six-tops with molded plastic chairs that made a scraping sound with each movement and laid a sort of uneven rhythm track beneath the babble of voices.

Samantha Early was at a table with three other girls. None of them were talking. Mason Crain, a pleasant-looking if not handsome kid who had not quite grown into his hands and feet, sat down across from her carrying a tray loaded with something brown, something green, and something red.

Samantha glanced up, then returned her gaze immediately to the laptop on which she was typing in between bites of turkey lasagna.

Two tables away sat Kayla and her friends. They were not all beauties, but even those who were of only average looks were well and expensively turned out, with better-than-Claire's jewelry, outfits from A&F and Nordstrom, designer shoes and bags and latest-generation cell phones.

"See who just sat down with Spazmantha?" Kayla asked.

All heads turned, noted the boy at Samantha Early's table, and looked back to Kayla for guidance as to why, precisely, this was important.

"That's Mason Crain," Kayla said. "He's acting all cool, but Samantha gave him a b.j. in his car up at the Headlands. In one of those pullouts where you can see the Golden Gate Bridge."

This in itself was not enough to elicit more than a few obligatory *eeeewww*s.

"Oh, my God," Kayla said in mock disbelief at their cluelessness. "Don't you know who Mason Crain's mother is?"

Publishing, I thought. His mother is in publishing. That fact must have come the same way so much came to me now, but for a moment I frowned, concentrating, trying to scroll back through my earlier encounter with Samantha's world, and I did not recall the moment at which I had heard that name.

Blank stares from Kayla's sycophants. Kayla waited for the suspense to build. "Mason Crain's mother is Amber Crain. She's a big deal, an editor or whatever they call them, at a big publisher."

The dots were still not connecting. So Kayla laid the last piece out in front of them, speaking slowly, as if to little children. "That's how she got her book published. Duh. Spazmantha sucked her way to success."

And now every eye turned back again to Samantha, and to Mason, but returning to Samantha. And from her seat Samantha must have felt the eyes on her. She looked up and saw six eager, malicious, titillated sets of eyes.

They made eye contact, six on one, and there was a burst of giggling, unmistakably directed at Samantha.

Samantha blushed, baffled by why exactly—why *this* time—she was being laughed at.

We moved again, in that seamless way that Messenger had of simply appearing where he wished to appear, and now we were with Samantha as she left school at the end of the day. She pulled out her cell phone and saw that her Twitter feed had lit up.

Twenty-nine tweets talking about her.

Some of them had a photo taken of her and Mason at lunch.

Samantha rocked back and for a moment looked as if she might faint. She leaned against her locker and scrolled again and again over the list of tweets, reading each of them, seeing new ones pop up. A thirtieth. A fortieth. In minutes the entire school would know a lie, a lie she could deny but never destroy.

Samantha gasped for breath. Her eyes darted to the exit, and she made a little jerking motion in that direction but couldn't seem to move. She was frozen in panic. Tears were filling her eyes.

I reached for her without thinking because her knees had started to buckle, but of course I could not touch her, I could not help her. Yet she needed help. Maybe there were people who could laugh off a rapidly spreading lie, but Samantha was not that person.

Kayla was coming down the hall with two of her followers, her primed-for-cruelty followers, her toadies, her co-conspirators. Not Kayla's fault alone, I thought, not just her—them, too! Them, too! They were laughing but not looking at Samantha, not making eye contact, *avoiding* eye contact, just laughing, loudly, with the hard-edged falseness that spoke of sadism and not humor.

Samantha looked almost pleadingly at Kayla. Not angrily—pleadingly, desperately. She looked like a cow going to slaughter who smells death ahead and knows with sickening dread that there is no escape.

"I don't want to watch this," I said. Minutes before I had been an unwelcome spy in Emma's and Liam's minds. Now I was a helpless witness to bullying. And I knew already where the bullying would lead.

It is a terrible thing to watch evil unfolding. It's a terrible thing to see doom coming to an innocent girl. I felt like throwing up. I felt sick of everything that had happened to me in the time since I had woken up beneath that unwholesome yellow mist. I crossed my arms, digging fingernails into my forearms, a protective pose, a fearful pose. A pose that in a small way transmitted reflected pain.

"How long?" I asked Messenger through gritted teeth. "How long have I been here?"

He did not answer.

"I can't do this," I said. I felt as if I couldn't breathe. As if my heart was too large an organ to fit my narrow chest. "You don't understand, I'm not like you. I'm not . . . I can't . . . I can't just watch this happen and not try to stop it."

"It's easier if you believe that all of this has already happened, Mara," Messenger said. There was something almost human in his voice. But I did not fail to notice his careful word choice.

Easier if I *believe*.

Had it already happened? It must have; I'd seen the final act of Samantha's tragic story. But what meaning did past and present and future have when you could dip in and out of a person's life, a minute here, an hour there?

It was impossible to accept as reality. But no, no, that wasn't quite true. In fact, I *had* accepted it. In a very short time I had adjusted in some ways at least to the notion that I could simply move through time and space. This new reality should not have been as easy to accept as a change in the weather.

I had a sudden realization.

"You closed off my memory to make it easier for me to adapt."

Messenger's face remained impassive. But something came through anyway, some sense that he was pleased. Pleased with me for understanding.

To my shame I swelled with pride. Then instantly I pushed that emotion away. Was I some lonely puppy, bouncing and groveling because Messenger had given me a pat on the head?

I called up the images I had seen when Messenger had touched me, images of terror and pain and utter despair. I could call him Messenger, but his full title was Messenger of *Fear.*

Fear. And I was to be his apprentice until such time as I was ready to become the dread messenger myself.

I imagined escaping from him. I could run out the door of this school and find a phone to call my parents. No, my mother. Just my mother. I had forgotten again that my father was dead.

I imagined the call. *Mom, I'm . . . somewhere. I need help. I'm trapped with a supernatural being who apparently thinks he's some sort of judge, jury, and executioner. Get me out of here. Wherever "here" is.*

I saw a memory of her then. Perhaps a memory of a picture. That simple gift, the ability to remember my mother's face, however imperfectly, filled me with emotion and made swallowing difficult.

I did not want to cry in front of Messenger, but I needed to cry for so many reasons. I needed to cry for Liam and Emma and the dog they had killed, and even for whoever might own and love that dog. I needed to cry for Samantha Early—I needed to scream at heaven for what was coming to Samantha Early.

And, in unworthy self-pity, I needed to cry for myself, because surely whatever I had done to deserve this, whatever had wrung soul-searing sobs from me, it must surely have been a mistake, an accident, like Liam and Emma. For surely whatever I had done, it was nothing that sank to Kayla's level. I didn't believe I was capable of true wickedness.

But I would learn that we don't always know ourselves.

I would learn that and more.

10

It was with the greatest relief that I saw we had moved on, leaving poor, doomed Samantha Early to read the 140-character mocks and insults and false expressions of disgust.

We stood outside a house perched just below a narrow, one-lane, poorly blacktopped and winding road. My house? For a moment it was almost as if Messenger had read my thoughts, my search for my own roots, and was taking me to a familiar place. There was a familiarity about the place, but no, of course this wasn't my house, it couldn't be.

"This is Kayla's home?" I asked, and received no answer. I was becoming accustomed to Messenger's taciturnity, to his grudging release of any information, as though truth was a poison that must be taken with the smallest of spoons, over time, allowing immunity to build up.

Kayla's family had money, that much was clear. The home was large, six bedrooms, with a pool to the side and a view of a stand of woods that might be inviting on the sunniest of spring days but now felt sullen, dense, and silent.

The slope behind the house was quite steep, even more sharply declined than the steps from the road down to the front door. That rear slope led down to Sleepy Hollow Creek. White alders, willows, and buckeyes grew tall, and the deck at the rear of the house was in the midst of those trees, so that sunshine only rarely struck the cedar planks and . . .

I blinked in confusion. I had not been to the back of the house—I was still standing on the road, looking at the house between parked cars. Was I now acquiring information without even the need to pose a question? Was I a fish swimming in a sea of information to which I had now, by virtue of my incredible situation, become entitled?

We stepped into Kayla's room, as though walking from the one-lane road directly into her room was a matter of course. There was an architecture, a geography to this sphere I now inhabited. I thought that eventually I must come to understand it if I was ever to free myself from an existence as a helpless appendage.

I could only wonder what my own home was like. The brief flashes of memory I'd enjoyed had given me very little to work with. I still had no idea what my room was like, but I felt sure it was not as nice as Kayla's.

She had a queen-size bed with an antique-white headboard detailed with a blue stripe that picked up the color on one of her walls. The other walls were lighter, avoiding the heaviness that can come from too much blue.

The furniture . . .

Wait a minute. I knew the furniture. That was a Restoration Hardware bed. The dresser and desk were both antiques. How did I know that? Why did I know that? I was too young to be some kind of interior

123

decorator. Was this an interest of mine? That would be an embarrassing bit of knowledge if it turned out I was a student of home furnishing.

I had felt from the start that I cared about words. Cared maybe too much, but that at least felt organic to me, part of me. This unusual knowledge of furniture must come from some personal experience. Maybe my own room had been redecorated?

I tried to force a picture to appear, but it would not, and my attention was drawn to Kayla, who was doing homework on her laptop, tapping, dragging her finger across the touch screen, tapping, glancing at a book, tapping some more.

Above her desk was a cork bulletin board, squeezed in between posters of pop stars and actors and a wistful travel poster from Venice. I moved in to see the bulletin board. A course list. A shopping list—very organized was our Kayla: eyeliner, socks, moisturizer, scrunchies.

My eye was drawn then to a ribbon, a blue satin rectangle with the letters "NaNoWriMo". I knew what it meant, which was both reassuring and unsettling. National Novel Writing Month. Kayla had participated, even won some sort of recognition.

The door opened. I fought back the instinct to hide. We were invisible, of course, except when Messenger decided otherwise. Through the door came a woman. She was pretty in a chrome-and-glass kind of way, cold, face unnaturally smooth, hair a glossy black, very different from Kayla. I was sure that black hair should be at least touched with gray, might have been so touched at some point in the past.

She was dressed in a too-short skirt and too-tight blouse over too-ambitious breast-enhancement surgery. She had the aspect of a woman trying very hard to be other than what nature had meant her to be.

"We're going out," the woman said.

Kayla didn't turn around. "You're supposed to knock."

"I don't need to knock in my own home."

"Your home. Of course," Kayla sneered. "Yours

and *his* now. Maybe he should be able to walk in on me without knocking, too. I'll bet he'd like to."

"Kayla, unless you have something to say, unless you have some kind of sensible thing to say, do not go there."

Kayla waved a dismissive hand and went back to her work, but she wasn't really reading; she was waiting, tensed and angry.

"Do you have something to say, Kayla?" her mother pressed.

"No, Jessica," Kayla said, her voice dripping with sarcasm. "Not at all. After all, I'm sure a man who is fifteen years younger than you, and only ten years older than me, has no interest at all in walking in on me."

Jessica crossed the room with long-legged strides, grabbed Kayla's shoulder, and spun her around. Kayla half fell from her chair and yelled, "Get out and leave me alone!"

"Listen to me, Kayla, if Arnie has done anything . . . questionable . . . you tell me. Otherwise, you stop spreading poison."

"Questionable? Has he done anything *questionable*? You mean, aside from moving into my house and sleeping with my mother in my father's bed?" Kayla's voice had risen with each word, louder, more insistent, and by the time she had reached the final syllable, there were tears in her eyes and her voice was a scream.

"I have a right to—"

"To sleep with whoever will have you?"

"You spoiled little—" Jessica snapped.

"Get your hands off me!"

"I am your mother, Kayla, whether you like it or not. I won't tolerate your disrespect."

"My mother? My mother wasn't a slut!"

"Watch your mouth!"

"I don't even want to be here. Oh, my God, I hate you! I wish Dad hadn't died!"

Jessica blinked and drew back. "Of course you miss your father, I—"

"Do not tell me that you miss him, too," Kayla said. Her tone was ferocious, a mix of anger and deep sadness. "He wouldn't . . . If you had died . . . he would never have . . ."

"He already was," Jessica said. As soon as the words were out of her mouth, she blanched, covered her mouth with one hand, and reached for Kayla with the other. Kayla slapped her hand away.

"What did you just say?" Kayla demanded. "What did you just say? *What did you just say?*"

"No one in this world is perfect or without failings, Kayla. Not even your father."

The room felt cold suddenly, the light gone grim and gray, as the two looked at each other. Kayla's face was red with anger; her eyes blazed through tears. Her mother was abashed but also, somehow, relieved of a burden.

"Go away," Kayla said. "This is my room."

"Kayla—"

"If he did, it was your fault!" Kayla said. "Now get out. Get out. Leave me alone."

At that moment the picture froze, though of course

it was no picture but a reality, an actual scene that must have played out in some corner of the time-and-space continuum Messenger so casually defied.

"What is the point of showing me that?" I asked Messenger.

"What do you think it is?"

"I don't know," I said, and I was none too deferential. I felt bruised by the confrontation I had just witnessed. Maybe it was normal in its own way; after all, mothers and daughters fought. I didn't know enough to judge who was in the right, or indeed whether they were both right or both wrong.

Messenger let time flow, so next I had to witness Jessica storming from the room and worse, see Kayla break down in tears.

She cried for a long time, deep, wracking sobs, the particular rhythm of a person who has suffered some terrible loss. I found I couldn't bear it. She was crying for her dead father, and I knew that I must have cried that same way, for that same reason. Perhaps I, too, had lashed out at those around me, unable to come to terms with my own feelings of unfairness and helplessness.

After far too long, Messenger said, "Good and evil are real. But the lines are seldom neat."

"Great, Obi-Wan," I said. "And what am I supposed to do with that?"

Messenger either didn't detect the sarcasm or didn't consider it worth addressing. He answered the question as though it had been sincere.

"The Messenger must understand," he said.

"Wonderful," I said, suddenly feeling exhausted. "So now I understand."

Messenger did not speak—he waited—and now Kayla was typing again. Not a Pages document but something on Facebook. A status update. I moved closer, curiosity overcoming the niceties of privacy, and read it over her shoulder.

Oh. My. God! she typed. *You will not even believe this. But I have a copy of Spazmantha's so-called manuscript. Okay, here's the love scene from page 102.*

She proceeded to type in an R-rated sex scene between a character named Jason and a girl named Sammie.

It was hastily written, but not so carelessly that it would set off alarm bells in a willing audience that so wanted it to be true.

It was explicit. It was humiliating. It was meant to sound as if it was a poorly disguised version of a sex scene between Samantha and Mason, the boy from the lunchroom. Kayla had some talent—that was the thing. She had enough talent to include some detail for verisimilitude. Enough talent to just about sound as if she was writing something that could be published, though her style could be stilted and overly dependent on polysyllabic words.

I glanced at Kayla's bookshelf and was not surprised to find Poe and Lovecraft amid the Roths and Greens and Krauses. Kayla had an interest in the gothic.

The Facebook posting sat there, long enough to be read, and then the "Likes" began to add up quickly. And then the "Shares."

Kayla switched to her Twitter feed and posted a pointer to her Facebook status. And those tweets were retweeted and favorited.

And just like that, the one thing Samantha Early had ever done that made her feel worthy and important was turned into a dirty joke.

Kayla included a sound that Samantha was supposed to have made.

That was the genius moment, I knew. I could practically feel Kayla's dark pleasure, knowing that this, above all, would be the knife to Samantha's heart.

Gurgle, gurgle, Sammie said.

It was silliness. It was false.

It killed Samantha Early.

"Consider what you have just witnessed," Messenger said. "Think on it, Mara, and come with me."

It sounded like an invitation, but of course it was no such thing. Before I could blink, we had left the now cold and remorseless Kayla behind and were once again with Liam and Emma.

11

"I offer you a game," Messenger said.

"What game?" Liam demanded.

Messenger would not explain. "If you win the game, you will both go free to consider what you have done. If you lose the game, you will suffer your greatest fear."

The two of them looked frightened already, like they'd already had plenty of fear, but I could see that Liam at least felt confident in his ability to win a game. Not cocky, but confident. Perhaps, I thought, he is an athlete accustomed to games, accustomed to competition, and has a justifiably high opinion of his abilities.

I hoped he was right. I didn't know then what Messenger meant when he warned of fear. But I was convinced that they deserved only the mildest of punishments.

I liked them; that was the truth of it. I liked that they

were in love. It made me wonder again whether I had someone about whom I cared that much. Was I in love, back in my life wherever? I doubted it, somehow.

And what of Messenger? What was that crack Oriax had made about Messenger and someone named Ariadne? No doubt someday when Messenger and I were sitting on a park bench, chatting and eating sandwiches while tossing crumbs to the pigeons, we'd come to that discussion. Hah. Not very likely, that scenario, though I would have liked to know more about him. Maybe there were things he could tell me that would explain away the awful imagery that contact with him had caused to flood my mind.

I squeezed my eyes shut, pushing that fleeting yet vivid memory away, just as I tried to push away memories of Samantha Early's end. It was ironic, I supposed, that I was simultaneously hungry for memories lost and terrified of memories I had come unwillingly to possess.

"We'll play," Liam said, jumping in to accept the wager before Emma could contradict him. Emma's breath caught and her eyes narrowed in irritation, but she subsided.

"If we refuse, we lose," Liam said. "If we play, we may win. Right?"

"You have accepted the game," Messenger intoned. He raised up his hands, palms out toward the two of them. Then, in a movement of such gravity that it could only be a ritual of some sort, he said, "In the name of Isthil, I summon the Master of the Game."

I very nearly burst out laughing, despite the queasy uncertainty that now defined my moment-by-moment existence. It seemed so like the self-serious, phony mysticism I might have expected from a Comic-Con attendee. That urge to laugh died unborn.

There came from the mist a sound, a scrabbly sound that a mouse—no, dozens of mice—might make racing across a tile floor. Then, beneath that sound, deeper, a noise like voices at a great distance, some crying, some, it seemed, as I strained to hear, like people talking fast and nervously.

These sounds, at once familiar and strange, grew louder as something moved through the mist. I peered into that hateful yellow miasma, anxious—or so I thought then—to catch a glimpse of this Master of the Game. Another Oriax, perhaps? Or a Daniel?

"Do not look into his eyes," Messenger said, his voice even nearer my ear, more intimate than before, as if this was what passed for a whisper from him.

The creature that slowly took form as the mist retreated reluctantly from him was tall, taller than any man I had ever seen. His skin was brown, like an old oak desk given a walnut stain. He might have been actual wood—a carved figure, a totem—but for the fact that he moved, long legs shuffling, giving an impression that his legs were too heavy to lift.

Heeding Messenger's warning, I kept my eyes on the parts of the creature that I felt were safest: hands, arms, legs, chest. He wore no clothing but needed none, as his entire body was of the same curiously grained wood. He might have been a mannequin or a puppet except for the size, and the sounds that now quite unmistakably emanated from him—though not from his head, nor from his as yet un-glimpsed mouth, but from the surface of his body, from the grain, from . . .

Not a grain, no; tiny channels, carvings into his brown flesh, like . . . And there I stopped breathing for a moment because I could not both see and digest what I was seeing and spare the focus required to breathe. Not a wooden grain but an endless maze carved into him, shallow runs that twisted and turned, forming suggestions of leering faces and twisted beasts. There was something Aztec there, something of demonic frescoes. These channels, this maze, it covered every inch of him. Within the channels were holes, black and sudden. It was not entirely rigid, this maze pattern, not entirely fixed, for there was movement there, down within those endless lines and curves and those baffling holes.

I heard more clearly now the sounds of what seemed like desperate scuffling feet and even, perhaps, though

I did want to believe it, fingernails scratching as if to escape, or to hold on. And the sounds of voices were ever more unmistakable as wheedling, begging, prayers almost, yes, and cries of despair.

Then as the last of the mist unveiled the full obscenity before me, I saw that things—living things—crawled in those maze tunnels. Human things. No bigger than cockroaches, they were nevertheless human, and they ran and staggered within that endless maze, indifferent to gravity, going up and down with equal ease or equal distress.

There were hundreds. Thousands, maybe. And some fell down the holes or maybe in extremis they jumped, and I knew then that this maze was not merely on the creature's skin but all the way through him. He was made of some precise wormwood, his entire body a mass of tunnels that might lead to places best not even to guess at.

And still I had not dared raise my eyes to his head, heeding Messenger's warning not to meet his gaze and now very much convinced, convinced down to the marrow of my bones, that I did not want to look in this monster's eyes.

But curiosity was as ever my weakness, though I had always believed it a strength. I followed a particular denizen of that maze as it ran upward, racing along with utter indifference to gravity the line of the creature's neck. I followed that scrabbling man, for man is what it seemed to me to be, as it ascended, and I used that focus as my excuse to myself for allowing my eyes to rise, inch by inch, along that twisted wood-hued form.

The man reached an ending and threw himself wildly against a barrier, but it was too late now for me to stop. I knew I would look higher. I knew myself that much at least—that I had no power to resist the terrible urge to know.

And so my dread-weighted eyelids rose and my neck craned and I saw the skeletal maw, the chipped and ragged teeth, as darkly stained as all the rest of the creature, and now, helpless to stop, I let my willful gaze travel up and ever up and then—

"No!" I cried, the word forced from a convulsing throat.

I turned sharply away but too late, too late by far. I had looked into the eyes of the Master of the Game and seen there the fleshy, swollen worms that gorged upon the insect-like humans.

"No, no, no, no, no," the voice said over and over again. My voice, though it was strained and unearthly. "No, no, no!"

I knew at that moment that all the pathways, all the tunnels, all the dark holes, the whole of the three-dimensional maze led inexorably to those eyes, to those worms, to that fate.

"Messenger," the Master of the Game said in a voice that creaked like sapling branches twisted to breaking. "Who are the players?"

For the first time since the appearance of the maze creature, I remembered the presence of Liam and Emma. All of my own horror was there written on their stricken faces. I felt obscurely guilty, as though I was somehow responsible for showing them this terrifying apparition. I saw in their eyes my own wonder and fascination mixed with revulsion. And worse, for they feared that they were to be reduced to lives as pitiable as the damned who lived within the Master of the Game. They saw themselves as those skittering, crying, helpless creatures trapped in tunnels and holes, lost, ever and ever lost in the maze.

And were they wrong? I didn't know. I had no words of comfort to give them. I had as yet no words of comfort for myself. And as Emma looked to me, she could see my own confusion and dread, and this amplified her own.

I did not look again at the monster's eyes. That was too much. That was a reality that had simply to be denied, pushed aside and forgotten if I was to maintain my slippery grip on sanity.

"These are the players," Messenger said. "Liam and Emma."

"One will play for both," the Game Master said.

I saw Messenger's eyes flick and his lips tighten. He didn't like that. It worried him.

"I'll play," Liam said, stepping forward protectively, imagining that he was being heroic, and that, I thought, was heroism, wasn't it? He had no idea what dangers might face him, and yet, looking at the Game Master, seeing the undeniably supernatural for the first time in his life, he somehow found it within him to push himself forward, to take on his fate.

But Emma was having none of it. "No, no, I'll do it!"

"Babe, no," Liam pleaded.

"I'm not going to let you deal with this by yourself, Liam."

They held each other, side by side, facing the Game Master. Messenger said, "Game Master . . ." But he stopped himself and took a deliberate step back.

"To each his own duty, Messenger," the Game Master warned. Then, to Liam and Emma, he said,

"The boy will play, but never fear, the female will have her own role."

"Step back, Mara," Messenger warned me. I obeyed.

The Game Master stood still, then raised his arms. From the blunt stubs where fingers should have been, there grew branches. These branches were leafless, crooked and gnarled, but lacking even the promise of life. They grew and spread to form a sort of bower, a nest or perhaps cage that surrounded and confined the two kids, who held hands throughout until, without willing it, they were simply apart, their own limbs seemingly paralyzed.

Messenger and I, outside this bower, watched.

"Do not attempt to interfere," Messenger said. "Whatever comes."

"Don't you know what is coming?" I asked.

"I am the Messenger of Fear. He is the Game Master. To each our own duty."

Something was growing like fruit from the unnatural branches. It bulged a sickly white blob that formed gradually into a flattened cylinder. Then upon one flat face of the cylinder, the pointed black hand of a clock. Just one hand. And just one number, at the top, where the twelve should have been. That number was zero.

While Emma, Liam, and I all stared at this odd fruit, something else was growing from the other side of the bower. It took the shape of hanging vines, six of them, as long as bullwhips.

"The game is a puzzle of twelve and one," the Game Master said. "Twelve pieces that must be assembled in one minute."

"Can't be too hard," Liam said with bravado that I prayed was not misplaced. "Where's this twelve-part puzzle?"

The cracked-tooth mouth smiled a skull's smile. "This is your puzzle."

At that the bullwhip tendrils erupted into life, whirling around Emma. It was no more than three seconds of mad flailing, with a noise like old-style Venetian blinds being thrashed.

The vines withdrew.

Emma's flesh and clothing alike were marked with red lines. She reminded me of charts I had seen in butcher's shops, of cows divided by roast and steak and rib.

She blinked. "Oh," she gasped.

Her arm, severed at the elbow, fell to the ground. No blood flowed. The severed end was a perfect, smooth, bloodless cross-section showing deep-red muscle, white ligaments, honeycombed pearl bone, a thin wrapping of tan flesh.

Her scream rose in her throat and Liam bellowed in fear, and the whips flew for a second time and a second piece dropped.

"Oh, God! Oh, God!" I cried, fists pressed to my mouth so hard I drew blood.

The whips flew and down dropped a hand, a leg, she toppled over and in mid-air was sliced in half at the waist, revealing organs cut through, intestines sluicing digested food that stopped as if by magic at the place where they were cut.

The pieces lay scattered. Eleven of them. An arm, a leg, a thigh . . . and Emma's head, mouth open in a soundless scream.

The pieces lay inert, all but that terrible, wordlessly, soundlessly screaming head.

A final slash of the vines, and Emma's head fell into two pieces like a split coconut, the halves rolling apart, both eyes on one piece, the mouth on another, the nose bisected.

I felt my knees collapse, and this time Messenger let me fall. I did not lose consciousness—I came to rest sitting on the cold ground, staring, mewling, my mind reeling back from the horror.

The vines descended, slowly now, like patient, stalking pythons, each looking for and finding a piece of Emma. Then, one by one, almost playfully, they threw the pieces into the bower, where they stuck like hellish apples hanging from a tree.

"Time starts . . . now," the Game Master said.

The clock hand began to move. It had passed the

place where the "2" would have been, and Liam still stood frozen, panicked.

"Liam! Move!" I shouted.

The Game Master hissed at me, like a cat, and his worm-filled eye sockets glowed with an eerie green light. But Liam sprang into action. He first took the two halves of Emma's head and, weeping and sobbing and with shaking hands, pressed the two pieces together.

Then pieces of torso, heavy as sandbags, slipping from his hands. He shoved and rolled the largest piece into the approximate space where it should be.

Already his time was half done.

"Hurry!" I urged, and in my anger at this horrible trickery, I looked the Game Master in the eye, defying him, cursing him even as I wept for Liam and Emma.

A thigh. A leg. A piece that was at first hard to place until it was rolled over and showed itself to be a hip.

Ten seconds left.

Leg to thigh. Arm to shoulder. It was like the children's song. *The knee bone's connected to the hip bone, the hip bone's connected to the . . .*

Five seconds!

Liam struggled with the two meaty chunks that would together form his love's upper torso.

Two!

Liam grabbed Emma's head and pushed it down against the severed neck.

A gong sounded.

No one breathed. I was sure even Messenger did not.

The Game Master said, "The player has won." He was, without any doubt, disappointed. But he maintained his monstrous dignity as the bower, that tangle of imprisoning branches, withdrew into his maze of a body.

Emma sucked suddenly at the air. She coughed. Liam bent over her on hands and knees and raised her up until she was sitting. He put his arms around her, and the two of them sobbed into the other's shoulder.

"Am I needed further?" the Game Master asked.

"No," Messenger said. "Not at this time."

"Have I performed my office?"

"Yes. You may withdraw."

The Game Master nodded. It was an almost amiable gesture. He stepped back and the mist wrapped around him, and he was soon gone from view. The sound of his captive creatures skittering and crying lasted for another few seconds and then faded beyond hearing, though not beyond memory.

"Stand," Messenger said to Liam and Emma.

I was amazed that they could manage it, and indeed it took some time. They seemed as stiff and weak as if they were very old people. But finally, helping each other, they stood erect, still holding hands, their faces masks of apprehension.

"You did wrong," Messenger said. "But you played the game and prevailed. You are free to go on with your lives."

"Are you kidding me?" Emma demanded. Her voice was shaky with the aftereffects of terror but powered by outrage. "You do that to us? You do that? And then—"

Liam cut her off. "He said we can go. Let's go."

Emma was not so easily silenced and lashed us with a furious onslaught of curses in both Spanish and English. But Liam managed to get her into the car, closed the door, and with a baleful look back at Messenger and, I suppose, me as well, started the engine and drove off into the night.

I am never without words, but I couldn't speak. Not then, not at that moment when I felt so utterly drained, so helpless and hopeless that I feared I would simply slip into unconsciousness.

"You are tired," Messenger said.

I was shaking too much to even nod my head.

"Yes, you need sleep. And food. We will go."

He watched me, saw my incapacity, the shock that reduced me to a near-paralytic state, and nodded.

"It is very shocking, the first time. You will grow more accustomed to it."

I wanted to tell him that the very idea of becoming accustomed to such foulness made me want to vomit.

I wanted to tell him that I would have no part of this, not now, not ever. I wanted to rage and beat my fists against his impassive face.

But he was no longer there.

I was in a bed.

The covers were pulled up to my neck.

My head rested on a soft pillow.

And sleep took me.

12

My dreams.

I don't want to speak of them—to speak of them, to relate the details, in some way makes them more real. I have decided to tell the truth here, as far as I can. But even as I determine to tell every detail, those details slip away, just out of my grasp. The dreams are like wraiths, like smoke, all incorporeal, all of it elusive as dreams so often are.

But as dreams will, they left behind a pall, a sense that in my sleep I had been victimized, my mind taken over by dark beasts that reveled in my fear and laughed at my dull efforts to snatch meaning from raw emotions.

I rolled out of the bed, examining everything around me as I did. Was this my bed? I had slept in it, but was it mine? Was this my room?

I touched the pillow thoughtfully. It was slowly

recovering from the weight of my head upon it. Was that fabric familiar to me? And this quilt. Was it mine?

The room was almost a square, with gray walls and a warm hardwood floor. A window shade allowed only the dimmest of light to sneak around its edges. A table lamp on the nightstand illuminated the contours of a desk and chair.

Slippers awaited my feet. Somehow I had been dressed for bed, though my last memory was of a heedless surrender to exhaustion. I wore soft, baggy shorts and a T-shirt. I pushed my fingers back through my hair, smoothing the few tangles. I wiped at my sleep-crusted eyes with the back of my hand.

There was a cork bulletin board over the desk. A blue ribbon hung there. I thought of looking more closely at it and learning whether it would tell me something of the reality or falseness of this place. This was not my bedroom. I had long since abandoned any faint hope that all of this was a dream. The dreams of my sleep were dreams, but what had happened with Liam and

Emma, with the Game Master, with Samantha Early, Oriax, and Daniel, all of that I now accepted as real.

Messenger was real, that taciturn but not completely emotionless creature whose careless touch had set off a cascade of horror but who was, for all of that, not truly wicked. Or so I reassured myself.

It was Messenger who had sent me to this bed. I would not call it "my" bed. It was Messenger who must have seen that I had reached my physical and mental limit. Maybe I should have blushed at the idea that he had undressed me and then dressed me as I now was, but I dismissed that notion. He was *not to be touched*. Surely his fingers on any part of my body would have awakened me screaming, no matter how deep the sleep.

There were three doors. One was almost certainly a closet. Another, I fervently hoped, was a bathroom. The largest door, the one most completely framed in painted molding, was surely the exit. I was nervous to check it, for fear that I would try the handle only to find that I was a prisoner.

MICHAEL GRANT

I nerved myself to try the closet. It was deep but not wide. Clothing was hung and shelved on the left side. There was an overhead light activated when I tugged on the string.

I sighed in disappointment: it all looked very much like the sorts of things a girl like Kayla would wear. Too fashionable, too adult for what I imagined my own tastes to be. I could not call up memories of my own closet or my own shopping preferences, but I had convinced myself that I was a simpler, more straightforward person than that. But when I pulled a top from its hanger, the immediate impression was that it was likely to fit me.

I gathered a few things and went to the bathroom, which was, to my great relief, a very normal bathroom. There was a toilet, quite welcome at that moment. And there was a shower, which was my next stop.

Has there ever been a better relief for stress and the effects of jading fear than hot water coursing through hair and over skin? I showered and shampooed and felt as if I might just stay beneath that comforting spray

156

until the hot water ran out. But it felt cowardly to hide away longer than necessary, or at least longer than I could justify.

I dried and dressed and stepped back into the bedroom. It was as I had left it. My eye was drawn to the posters on the walls, the same, it seemed at a superficial glance, as those on Kayla's walls. Presumably Messenger, or whatever other creature of his had made this place, had relied on those images to create the layout and decorations.

I was suddenly aware that I was dying of hunger and thirst. No food magically appeared, which meant that I must risk the final door. I approached it with my heart beating too fast and my breath too slow, convinced that opening it would reveal my imprisonment.

But when at last I nerved myself up and threw open the door, I saw there only a mundane hallway with another room at the end of it, a room of which I could see only a sliver but which looked very much like a kitchen.

Down the hallway I went, dressed in clothing that I was convinced was not mine but which nevertheless fitted me perfectly, at least in terms of size if not in terms of character.

The apparent kitchen was indeed a kitchen. Sun-dappled leaves rustled softly just beyond the window. A bowl of fruit sat on a butcher-block island. A loaf of bread sat unopened.

I seized greedily on an apple, bit into it, and drew open the refrigerator door. Yogurt. Milk. Cold cuts and condiments. A dozen eggs and a package of bacon. Butter and orange juice and cranberry juice, too, because my mother believed it protected against infections.

I ate the apple, found cereal in the cabinets, ate some of that as well, and then fried an egg, which I ate with toast.

I felt much better after eating. If a warm shower is the greatest of comforts, then surely wholesome food is the second greatest. Something in the simple rituals of composing my meal gave me reassurance that I had some small degree of control over my life.

I wondered if I should clean up after myself. Had Messenger summoned a helpful maid from the collection of allies and opponents he appeared to have? Would any such maid be a monster, like the Game Master? Or perhaps a transcendent beauty like Oriax? I managed a laugh at that notion, an honest laugh that sent me wondering whether I was in fact resilient enough to endure whatever might yet come my way.

Just one thing remained: to open the beckoning door to the back deck, step out into the sunshine I saw through the window.

I cleaned up after myself, placing my trash in the bin and my dishes in the dishwasher. Then I grabbed a peach and a paper towel to absorb any juice, and opened the door to the deck. As I twisted the knob, it occurred to me that something had been missing from the bedroom and the hallways leading to the kitchen: Wouldn't there be family photographs somewhere in one or both locations? But I was unwilling to backtrack.

I wanted to exploit my temporary sense of well-being to push on further, servant as always to my curiosity.

I opened the door, and where the leafy deck might be, there stood Samantha Early.

13

"I can't go to school. I'm sick."

For a moment I thought Samantha was talking to me. She was looking right at me, and since I had just come through the door, there was no way she could be speaking to someone behind me.

"What?" I said. She did not respond and I heard then a second voice. Impossibly, it was behind me. I spun and saw that the kitchen, the one I had just been in, was gone, as was the house. As well as the peach that had been in my hand.

Instead we were in a driveway. A Ford SUV was warming up, tailpipe purring smoke and steam, a man in the driver's seat, a chubby man with pleasant features, a receding hairline, a blue-striped dress-shirt and loose tie. He had a travel mug of coffee in his hand.

"Oh, come on, Sammie, you've skipped the last two

days. This is going to start affecting your grades."

Self-conscious, I moved to get out from between the two of them, though of course I was invisible to them.

"Dad, I really don't feel . . . It's my time of month. I have cramps."

The father looked as uncomfortable as fathers will when such things are discussed, but he shook his head and said, "Come on, Sam, grab your backpack and let's go. I have a staff meeting first thing and there's construction on the 101."

The 101? That phrase struck a chord with me, but no doubt that road went all over the country and—

"Will she go to school, won't she go to school—the suspense is killing me." The intimacy of the voice combined with the highly charged sensuality that somehow permeated the flippant tone told me instantly that Oriax was with me. I turned eagerly to see her.

She was dressed differently this time, still exotic, still sporting the sort of leather outfit that would not have been out of place on a female superhero, but with less black and more green. And an amulet had been added to a green ribbon choker around her throat. It was a jewel, as big as a cherry tomato, but of a rich green color that held sparkling starlight within.

She saw me staring at the jewel—the emerald, I supposed it was, though if it was real, it would cost Samantha's father's yearly salary. "You like?" Oriax asked me.

"It's beautiful," I said.

"You should get one," she said. I thought she was preparing to remove it and hand it to me, but then her eyes flicked to my right and she lowered her hands. "There you are, Messenger. I was wondering why you'd leave poor . . . What's your name again?"

"Mara," I said.

"Messenger-in-waiting," Oriax said. It was a sneer, but as she said it, she winked at me so I didn't take it amiss. "Has he told you the big reveal yet?"

"The big what?" I asked. I felt rather dull, but then I was destined to feel rather dull in her company.

"Leave us, Oriax," Messenger said.

"Not just yet, Messenger," she said. She turned languidly away from me as Messenger moved closer. "It's not a done deal, and you know it. She may still choose to come with me, to follow the path of . . ." She pouted, thinking of just the right word before finishing with, ". . . excitement."

"She's not for you, Oriax, or for your mistress. She's chosen her path. She will stay on it."

Were they discussing me? As if I was some object to be bartered or sold? Hadn't Oriax just mentioned a choice? Did I have a choice? What was the nature of that choice?

"I think you're wrong, Messenger," Oriax said, and there was an edge to her voice now. "I think she's demonstrated that she could be very useful to us. Very happy with us. You forget: I know all that she does not."

I don't know why I reacted so strongly to that. Maybe it was just the idea that Oriax knew me, that she knew who I was, all of what I was, or at least more than

I knew. I reached out instinctively and touched her arm.

When I had touched Messenger, I had been deluged by terrifying images of pain, fear, loathing, and despair. In touching Oriax, I unleashed a similarly intense flood of imagery, but . . . oh, the intensity and the suddenness were all the two experiences had in common. For these were not images of pain but of pleasure.

What a pale word. *Pleasure.* What a vanilla word, for the overpowering flood of sweating, grunting, delirious physical sensuality. My mouth hung open in shock. I did not like to think that I was naive, but whatever I had guessed or intuited of the body's capacity for raw experience, it was nothing that began to approximate what Oriax's touch had revealed.

I was embarrassed and overwhelmed. I was repelled and yet . . . not just repelled. My mouth was dry, my eyes wide, my heart pounding, and there were other sensations, sensations that I had never before felt but which nevertheless touched some chord in me.

"Oh!" I said.

"Do you see, Messenger? She said, 'Oh!' Don't you want to savor the sweet innocence in that single syllable? 'Oh!'" Oriax laughed. It was not a good laugh. Yes, it was musical, yes, it was delightfully rich and deep, but it struck some discordant note, too.

I drew back a step, and I could see that this unconscious reaction irritated Oriax. Her eyes snapped to Messenger, an oddly reptilian movement, too quick to be human. A predator's eyes.

Messenger said, "You have the right to make your offer, Oriax."

"Oh, not just yet, I think," Oriax said, no longer in such a playful mood. "We will talk again, when she comes to see the whole truth and faces what her fate must be with you, Messenger. Then." She raised one exquisitely manicured finger, extended it slowly, and let it merely brush my cheek.

I shuddered as the images washed through me again, washed through me but did not leave me feeling clean. But I closed my eyes, and I . . . savored them . . .

just for a moment before they faded away. I knew before I opened my eyes that she would be gone, and she was.

Messenger watched me with the detachment of a scientist watching a specimen in a petri dish.

"What choice?" I asked him.

He looked at me, looked directly into my eyes, and I felt powerless to do anything but return his gaze. His detachment grew strained and I felt that, in some way still too inchoate to explain, he was giving me something, some curse or blessing. Or maybe it was all my imagination, so recently rocked by Oriax.

But for just a moment I saw things in his blue eyes. There was power there, and loss. There was knowledge but also vulnerability. He was, for all his strangeness, a boy. Maybe he was a thousand years old. But maybe he was barely older than me. Beneath that long black coat with its dreadful skull buttons, and beneath that severe, steel-gray shirt, there was maybe something real, something physical.

167

He was not a spirit, I felt, but a real being, a person, a mind but also a body.

But no, all of this was just a sort of hangover from the wild fantasies Oriax's touch had revealed. No, I told myself harshly, you must not forget, Mara, that this boy is in league with the Master of the Game and that his touch was the very soul of darkest terror.

Samantha Early had fetched her backpack. She was going to school. Only after she had climbed into the car with her harried father did I recognize that she was wearing the exact outfit in which she killed herself.

"Oh, God. It's today," I said.

"Yes," Messenger said.

"We have to . . . to stop it."

I expected a non-answer or at best a cryptic comment that would do nothing to reassure or enlighten me. But, to my surprise, Messenger came closer and waited until the gravity he exerted had brought me to face him, to look at his face, into his eyes.

"You must understand. We do not have the duty

of changing the world, of substituting our own wills for those of the people involved. A human deprived of freedom becomes something less than human. There must be free will. Even when . . ." Some dark memory clouded his eyes and caused him to glance away, as if to hide a pain he was unwilling to reveal. He took a steadying breath and in a monotone went on, "People are free to make choices, even terrible ones. But when they make bad choices, when they do evil, then it may be that justice, fairly and ruthlessly applied, can show a person a new path. Justice is our cause, not human happiness."

I was torn as to what to say in response. This was the most Messenger had ever shared with me. I didn't want to discourage future explanations with too many questions, let alone arguments.

But just as curiosity drives me, so a lesser attribute, argumentativeness, sometimes rears its head. So I said, "If the point is justice, why the game? Why not just decide a sentence and carry it out?"

I blushed to see what next animated his face, for I was certain that for just the briefest moment, a flash that escaped before he could conceal it, he had looked at me with affection. Once he had recomposed his features into their usual emotionless character, he said, "Here is what I have been taught, and a small part of what I must teach you."

Then he drew four circles of light. They hung in the air. I noted my own calm reaction to what was at the least a very convincing special effect or at most something very like a miracle. I had seen nothing but miracles since waking in a field of dead grass beneath a sentient mist.

The circles were blue, red, green, and a color that I could not name, since it appeared to shift, never remaining anything identifiable.

"This," he said, touching the blue circle, "is what you are given at birth: your physical self, including your brain." Messenger next touched the red circle. "Here is what you have lived: your parents, your schooling, all that you have seen and felt in your sixteen years. Your experience."

He drew the red circle across so that it partly overlapped the blue.

"This," he said, touching the green circle, "is your free will, the decisions you make." He drew this circle across to overlap the earlier two.

Then he waited, no doubt knowing that curiosity would compel me to ask, "And the final circle?"

"This?" He touched the variegated circle. "This is chaos and randomness. It is chance."

He pulled this final circle into position so that it overlapped the configuration, touching what I was given, what I had experienced, and my free will in turn. At the very center of the pattern, the overlapping circles formed a bulging rectangle. He touched it and it glowed with a bright-white light.

"And that," Messenger said, "is you. And me. And Samantha and Liam and Emma, and all human beings. We live our lives in a shifting matrix of what we are given, what we experience, what we choose, and what random chance does that we cannot control."

"The game is randomness," I said.

"The game is randomness," he agreed. "It is the most ancient of forces. In the beginning was a moment when random chance turned nothing to something. Nonexistence to existence."

I had many more questions, and, perhaps sensing this, Messenger moved us, so that we were no longer in Samantha Early's driveway but once more in her school, standing, as Samantha herself was, beneath the banner that read: *Congratulations Samantha On Your Suck-cess!!!*

It is possible that a stronger person—a person less wracked by the self-doubt that comes hand in hand with the cruel loss of control of compulsion—might have found a way to laugh it off. Even as fingers were pointed, and cruelly comic faces were made, and braying laughter filled the hallway. It is possible that another person could have somehow found the strength to hold her head high even as the one success she had ever had in her life was discredited, ridiculed, and reduced to ashes.

But Samantha Early was not that person.

Kayla, alone for once, watched from behind her open locker door. I saw her there. I saw her eyes follow Samantha as she dropped her book bag, turned, and fled the school, chased away by sickening gales of laughter.

Kayla had triumphed absolutely.

14

I wanted to kill her. Kayla. I didn't know the girl, had never guessed at her existence until the day before. But I felt a sickness inside myself watching her in her victory, her pointless, cruel victory.

"Call the Game Master," I said through gritted teeth.

Messenger said nothing. He was back to his taciturnity, his . . . I was about to say indifference, but when I saw his face, what I saw there was not indifference. He was looking at me with pity, as though he regretted my words. Or perhaps as though he was sorry to have made this tragedy a part of my life.

"She deserves to be punished," I said stridently. "She killed Samantha as surely as if she'd stabbed her with a knife."

Messenger looked at me for a long time, as if considering what he should do with me. What I had taken earlier for approval, and then pity, had turned flinty. But whatever he was planning to do next was stopped by the arrival of Daniel, who walked past Kayla and beneath the banner. In his casual clothing he looked almost as if he could be one of the students now rushing to disappear into their classrooms.

"Daniel," Messenger said in curt greeting.

"Messenger," Daniel said just as curtly. "A matter requires your attention."

"Another case?"

Daniel nodded. "A very serious one, I am sorry to tell you."

"I am with my apprentice," Messenger said tightly.

"Your apprentice is meant to learn, is she not?"

"I would soften the shock with a bit more time," Messenger said.

"You have a soft heart, Messenger. I admire your compassion. But we have our obligations. We do not serve ourselves, or even our apprentices."

From that statement—delivered in a clipped,

no-nonsense style—I learned two things: that I had been mistaken in seeing Daniel as easygoing, and that for whatever unfathomable reason, Daniel saw Messenger as softhearted. It made me want to laugh. The Messenger of Fear might have moments of compassion, but he had summoned the Game Master to terrify Liam and Emma, and if that had been compassion or softheartedness, it was of a type so attenuated that I could hardly recognize it.

"Oriax has her eye on my apprentice," Messenger said. "I wish to take the necessary time to prepare her."

"Oriax and her folk are always busy, as you know. It is possible that while Oriax teases you, Messenger, knowing your vulnerability she has been at work elsewhere."

Messenger drew a sharp breath. He had not liked the implication that Oriax had an effect on him. "So long as Ariadne lives, Oriax will have no power over me."

Daniel sighed, looked down, and shook his head, a bit like a disappointed parent. "Don't be a fool,

Messenger. Do as you are directed. You see a great deal. But you do not see all."

At that, Daniel, with a sideways glance at me, laid his hand against Messenger's cheek. Strange to me that there could be something parental in that touch, for Daniel was smaller than Messenger. Perhaps a few years older, but in no way imposing or impressive.

I wondered whether Daniel, when he touched Messenger, who was not to be touched, saw that same horror show of images that still rattled like skeletons around in my mind.

The contact lasted for at least a minute, and halfway through Messenger bowed his head in acceptance. I was sure that Daniel was telling him something, transferring information of a sad nature to him, for Messenger's eyes drooped and closed, and a weary sigh rose from his chest.

Finally Daniel took his hand away and Messenger stood there, silent, eyes still closed, rocking almost imperceptibly back and forth.

Daniel looked at me, waited until he was certain that he had my full attention, and said, "He is your master. You are his apprentice. Learn from him. He is a very good teacher." He paused, gazing up at Messenger, as sad now as my "master", and added in a husky voice, "He has given great service, and he has endured more of this wicked world than I hope you ever shall."

Daniel walked around the two of us, and when I turned to watch him go, he was already gone. Kayla, too, was gone, though whether to her next class or elsewhere, I did not know.

"We must go," Messenger said.

"Go? But aren't we going to deal with Kayla?"

He shook his head. "She has already been . . . dealt with. This new thing—"

"She hasn't been dealt with," I said hotly. "She hasn't had anything happen to her. You put Liam and Emma through hell for nothing. Okay, not nothing, but they were good people, not a wicked, manipulative bitch like Kayla."

His answer was sharp and angry. "Be silent, or you will regret your careless words later."

And then, in the usual Messenger style, we were gone from Samantha Early's school. Though not from her story.

I would learn more of Samantha and Kayla, much more, and I would cry bitter tears over that final chapter.

15

The next thing I saw was a cage with chipped-paint steel bars. That cage was large enough to contain eight long steel tables bolted to the bare concrete floor, a television mounted on one wall, two filthy, open cinderblock-walled bathroom areas. It was also large enough to comfortably hold three dozen men, and was at the moment holding twice that number.

The men ranged in age from their fifties down to their teens. Each was dressed in an orange jumpsuit, though there were variations within narrow limits: some wore the jumpsuit with sleeves down to cover track marks; others wore the sleeves rolled up to show off tattoos. Some had their zippers down to their navels, others had peeled the top off entirely to let it hang loose, still others were zipped up tight.

It was not difficult to see that the day room of the

Contra Costa County Jail in Martinez was divided along racial lines. African Americans occupied the closest tables, Latinos took the next group, and white prisoners, many sporting Nazi tattoos, were farthest away and smallest in number.

Food had been served. Bologna on white bread, canned peaches, something that might once have been broccoli. Men ate with plastic forks, their shoulders hunched forward, their heads low over their food. The room was ear-splittingly loud from the television, which showed a mixed martial arts match that earned catcalls, groans, and shouts, as well as a more generalized yelling, guffawing, and even, here and there, unimpressive attempts at singing or rapping.

Messenger stepped through the bars. I watched him as he did it, suspecting he would do so, and wanting to observe closely to better understand just how he performed this particular bit of magic. But again, it was as if my eyes were simply not adapted to seeing what was happening before them. The closest I could come to describing it is to say that the bars seemed to avoid Messenger.

He motioned me forward, and though I had by that point walked through more than one solid object, I hesitated. I might have been invisible to the inmates, but that was a knowledge that did not reach down with so much certainty that it could easily override my natural caution. Put plainly: the men in there frightened me. It was a mundane, real-world, and thus all the more compelling fear, different from the fear of the supernatural evoked by something like the Game Master.

But when Messenger jerked his head impatiently, I followed, and my fear of the men distracted me so that I scarcely noticed that I was once more suspending the laws of physics and passing through case-hardened steel bars.

Messenger moved on to stand across from a particular young man, an African American, maybe seventeen but maybe fifteen, it was hard to tell. He was tall but not muscular, good-looking without rising to the level of handsome. His most notable feature were his eyes, which were large and luminous, a light brown at odds with his dark skin.

He was afraid. He was shaking. He was chewing the bologna sandwich in a dry mouth, mechanically working his jaws as two men, one to either side, leaned in far too close, pressing muscular biceps against him. Squeezing him and looking past the boy to wink at each other, to laugh conspiratorially.

"His name is Manolo," Messenger said.

"He's too young to be in here."

"Yes. But even the young are sent here when they are accused of murder."

I looked at Manolo with new eyes, searching for something to connect with that most terrible of crimes. Murder? He was a scared boy.

"You going to eat them peaches, boy?" one of the thugs asked.

Manolo couldn't speak—his mouth was full—so he

nodded yes and hunched closer around his food.

"Hear that, G? This young man wishes to eat his peaches."

"Huh."

The first inmate stuck his hand out to Manolo. "I'm Andrews. What they call you?"

Manolo stared at the hand, then reluctantly shook it. "Manolo."

"Oh, that is a weak handshake, little brother. That is a limp handshake, Mamomo. Yeah."

"Manolo."

"Yeah. Mamomo. That's what I said."

"Mamumu?" the other inmate mocked, his voice thick to the point of incomprehensibility. He laughed and slapped his hand down hard on the steel table. "Mamumu ma ma, moo."

"You a sword swallower, Mamomo?"

Manolo shook his head.

Andrews leaned in closer. "Nah, I think you are. That weak handshake there? You all scared. All shaking.

Hey, that's okay, you're a fish, you maybe ought to be scared—there's some bad men in here. Like Carolla here. He's a bad man, aren't you, Carolla?"

"Bad man," the other one confirmed.

"See," Andrews said. "You need to make friends fast here, fish. Need someone to watch your back."

Carolla stuck his hand into Manolo's plate, scooped up a peach slice, and popped it into his mouth.

"See? There you go. You let Carolla eat your peaches, maybe he won't hurt you. If you don't be nice, he's going to hurt you. He'll knock the teeth out of your mouth and bust you open, that's a fact."

Manolo swallowed, stiffened, and tried to stand up, but both men grabbed his shoulders and slammed him down hard into his seat. Both men began eating his peaches, making a joke of it, slurping and slopping, while Manolo sat helpless, pinioned.

"Let me go!" Manolo yelled.

Andrews put a hand behind Manolo's neck and slammed his face down into his tray. When his head came back up, there was blood pouring from his nose.

All the while I was growing increasingly uncomfortable. I told myself that this boy was a murderer—that he had taken a life and therefore deserved none of my pity. But even a less active imagination than my own would have seen where this was heading, what these two brutes intended for him. I did not wish to see it.

"Do we have to watch this?" I demanded.

"Don't you want to alter the fabric of time to rescue him, as you wished to do for Samantha Early?"

"It's not the same," I said through gritted teeth. "Samantha is just a victim. This boy killed someone. But that doesn't mean I want to watch him . . . like this." A thought occurred to me. "He did kill someone, right?"

"Yes," Messenger confirmed.

"Then, do we have to summon the Game Master and all of that?"

"Manolo is not our charge. We are after another one."

"Then, why are we here watching this?" I demanded,

quite angry, feeling that I was being tricked.

The room froze. One second it was a brutal and threatening video; the next it was as still as a photograph. And then, it began to move in reverse. Regular speed at first, with movements that seemed oddly normal, though backwards. Then the actions sped up, faster and faster so that we were standing in a swirl of orange jumpsuits and then an interrogation room with tired cops seeming to wave their hands at Manolo as he went from tears to sullen defiance, to his own hand-waving defiance.

On and on it went, out of the police station, into a squad car, back through a drive across a city I did not recognize, and slower then as red and blue strobes flashed and neon rippled across the wet skin of police cars in the rain, and then were gone.

The action backed past something that happened in a flash, then slowed, stopped, and began to move forward again in normal speed.

Manolo, no longer in jailhouse orange, was walking

out of a fro-yo shop. He wore a name tag, so I assumed he was leaving a part-time job. The fro-yo was at an aged mall with a sparsely occupied parking lot. The lot was illuminated by the worst of security lamps, which cast a silvery light, like moonlight drained of all mystery. Manolo walked toward his car, a beater sedan he must have inherited or perhaps saved his money to buy.

Two boys climbed from an SUV parked nearby. The boys were not particularly tough-looking. They were almost identically dressed in jeans, T-shirts, and jackets. One wore tan work boots, the other sneakers. Two things marked them instantly as dangerous. First, the way they moved: quick, almost hurried, directly toward Manolo, but furtive as well, with many glances behind and to the sides.

Second, they were each armed. Boots carried a metal baseball bat. Sneakers had a crowbar, hooked at one end, tape-wrapped at the other, which formed the grip.

Manolo was no fool—he knew as soon as he heard

their car door shut that he was in trouble. It was easy to see that he knew the boys.

He tried to get the car door open, but they afforded him very little time, and his first attempt to insert the key failed.

Had he managed to get the door open . . . Chance. The fourth of the forces that define our lives.

"Hey, guys, come on," Manolo said.

I noticed then that he had a bruise under one eye, and that a discreet flesh-colored bandage lay across his nose.

' "Come on?" ' Sneakers asked. "What do you mean 'come on,' faggot?"

"You already beat on me for no good reason!"

"Yeah, I seem to recall that," Sneakers said. "You got us both detention for that."

"That wasn't even the worst part," Boots said angrily. "Sensi—what did they call it?"

"Sensitivity and awareness," Sneakers said with a sneer. "An hour-long video. Plus the counseling. See,

Manolo, you gotta pay for all that. It's not just you being a homo—you were a homo who ratted us out."

"That's extra beating."

"That's blood. And something broken. And maybe a dead faggot," Sneakers said.

Manolo cried and tried again to insert the key. Boots grabbed his hand, crushing the keys in his grip. Manolo yanked his hand away, and Boots smashed the fat end of the baseball bat into his solar plexus.

Manolo lost every atom of air in his lungs, clutched his stomach, and sagged into the side of his car.

"That hurt, homo? Did that hurt?" Sneakers gave him a shove with the crowbar, sending Manolo staggering into the other attacker.

"What, you think you eyeball me in the shower and all you get is one beating?" Boots demanded.

"I didn't . . ." Manolo squeezed the words out but could say no more.

"Are you saying he's not good-looking enough for you, faggot?"

"I think he's dissing me," Boots said, picking up on his companion's snark. "Except we know better, don't we? Because I saw him watching me. Yeah. And the more I think about it, one little beating is just not enough."

"Just let me go . . . My mom . . . Someone will see you," Manolo said. He had his elbows down to guard his sides and stomach, while keeping his hands up, scrunching down to guard his head.

Sneakers swung the crowbar into the back of Manolo's legs.

"Ahhh!" Manolo cried. "Ahhh. Ahhhh!"

"Cry, you pussy!" Boots said. He shouldered his bat, just as if he was at home plate waiting for a fastball. He swung at shoulder height, cutting slightly upward, aiming squarely for Manolo's head.

Manolo ducked. The bat ruffled his hair as it flew past and smashed into Sneakers's cheek. The sound of breaking bone was as loud as a firecracker, followed by a howl of pain from Sneakers, who dropped his crowbar to grab his face.

"Dude!" Boots yelled.

"Ow ow ow ow!" Sneakers cried as tears filled his eyes.

Manolo tried to run but tripped over Sneakers's feet and landed hard on the blacktop, elbows and knees.

Boots cursed furiously and aimed a hasty blow that punched into Manolo's kidney, bringing new cries of pain to join those still pouring from Sneakers.

"I will kill you! Kill you, you—" Boots raised his bat again, but Manolo lashed out desperately and drove a foot against Boots's knee, and the bully staggered back.

In a flash Manolo had rolled over, powered to his feet, and come up holding the dropped crowbar.

Boots saw it and grew wary. "Oh, you want to throw down, faggot? I was just going to beat you. Now I'm a kill you! You hear me?"

Sneakers rallied and came rushing in a murderous rage to hit Manolo from behind with a flying tackle that drove him into Boots. The three of them went down in a tangle of fists and feet and elbows, all yelling, crying, cursing, and then somehow Manolo was up again, still holding the crowbar. His breaths came in furious gasps, loud, almost musical, and he swung the crowbar down once, hard, hitting Sneakers and shattering his collarbone.

Boots was trying to get to his feet while still holding the bat, but he was too slow and Manolo caught him with a hard, horizontal blow that broke his elbow. The bat went twirling off across the parking lot.

An adult male voice yelled, "Hey, hey! We've called the cops!" I glanced over and saw a youngish married couple next to their car, watching cautiously.

But Manolo was in no condition to hear anymore. He was in a rage. He was pure, distilled fury. He swung the crowbar again, and this time the thick steel bar landed with a horrible crunch on Boots's head.

Boots stopped trying to stand.

Manolo hit him again, and now blood was pouring down Boots's face, and Manolo hit him again as the woman from the couple yelled, "Stop it, stop it, you're killing him!"

And he was.

Manolo hit him three more times, sobbing as he did it, cursing, spitting down into the jellied mass that was his tormentor's head.

I had no time to prepare for or ward off the physical reaction that took hold of me, forcing me to bend over and vomit onto the pavement.

How can I explain that reaction, except to say that I had never witnessed anything as violent before. Samantha Early's death had been awful beyond anything I had seen up to that moment, but I had known it was coming. I saw it coming. It had about it an air of stateliness, almost, of inevitability. I was prepared.

I had no preparation for the animal frenzy that had erupted before me. I had never heard the sound of steel thudding again and again onto meat and bone. And all of it had happened so very quickly that I had no time to shift my sympathies. For at first I was happy that Manolo had prevailed. Mere seconds passed from that emotion to the physical rejection of the brutality I saw following.

I heard a siren. I saw flashing lights.

Manolo searched the ground for his keys, but his eyes were filled with tears and his mind was deranged by the most desperate feelings of pain and anger, regret and savage triumph, all mixed together.

In the end he just leaned back against the car—panting, spent. I heard the crowbar clatter to the ground. I heard Sneakers whining and saying, "He broke my face, he broke my face," over and over again.

"Tell me, Mara: What do you see here?"

I was still wiping my mouth and trying to gather my wits, trying to focus. Messenger's cold-sounding question was hard at first even to comprehend. But I understood that this was some sort of test, and because I am ever the striver looking to excel, even when the object of the game is something I reject, I did my best to answer.

"He defended himself. Lost it. Oh, my God, killed

that boy." I took several deep breaths, tried vainly to slow the jackhammer insistence of my heart. "Is that the murder Manolo's in jail for? He was defending himself!"

"Manolo's fate is for human agency to determine. His doom will be pronounced by a jury and a court."

I stared at Messenger in part because it was easier than watching the tragedy unfolding before us as Manolo was handcuffed, weeping, and Sneakers was taken away in an ambulance, his face swathed in bandages.

"We're not here for Manolo?"

He shook his head.

Slowly it dawned on me. Manolo was in jail. Boots was dead. There was only one other.

"The other boy. The one in the sneakers."

"The dead boy's name is Charles," Messenger said. "We are here for Derek. Derek Grady. Because as surely as Manolo, Derek is responsible for this death, yet he will not be arrested and he will not see any justice . . . but that which we deliver to him."

16

We took a stroll through Derek Grady's life, much as we had done with Samantha. After an exhausting and dispiriting time of it, Messenger took us away to a place I'd never been but that I knew instinctively was important to my taciturn teacher.

My first thought was that Messenger had taken time travel to a whole new level. We were high atop a massive stone wall of such ancient creation that it was topped with crenellations and interrupted by slate gray-roofed conical towers.

Looking inward from the wall, I gazed across red-tile roofs, limestone walls, streets so narrow they could never have been meant for carriages, let alone cars. The wall curved far in both directions, enclosing this small village.

Gazing out from the wall, I saw a lazy river passing

beneath an arched bridge of the same stone and vintage. But beyond that river was a much larger town, one still very much marked by history, but with cars and buses visible, as well as satellite dishes and the other usual indicators of the modern era.

I turned away from that and studied the village within the walls and saw that here, too, were the signs of modernity, though less obvious: people talking on cell phones, electric lights shining from within narrow windows, tourist souvenirs spilling from the low doorways onto tight streets.

"Carcassonne," Messenger said. Then, seeing my blank expression, added, "France."

"Why . . ."

Messenger was peering down at the street, not with the casual appreciation of a tourist but rather like someone looking for something very specific. Hopefulness and wistfulness momentarily defined his features, until he composed himself and regained the impassivity he wore as a mask.

"It's beautiful, don't you think?" he asked. "We see a great deal of pain. Beauty can be an antidote."

It made sense, almost. But I didn't believe him. He wasn't here for a change of scenery. He was looking for something. Or someone.

"Tell me what you learned of Derek Grady," he said, continuing to peer down into the town as he began to walk. He had long legs and walked quickly, in a hurry, searching. I had to rush to catch up. We were not alone on the wall—tourists passed by speaking half a dozen different languages—but as with doors and prison bars, they seemed to subtly relocate to avoid touching us. I was sure that we were quite invisible and inaudible.

"Derek's a bully," I said, thinking Messenger wanted the same economy of words from me that he practiced himself.

"More," he said.

"Okay, he's . . . well, he has a hard time in school, maybe because he doesn't study very hard and maybe because he's not very bright. He's on the wrestling team, along with Boots . . . That's what I call the other boy, the one who died."

"Charles," Messenger said with a flash of anger. "Charles Francis Frohlick. That's the name of the dead boy, a boy who was a bully and who may have grown up to be a worse bully, maybe a killer, even. But who might also have grown up to repent and change and to add something positive to this sorry world."

"Charles," I said, abashed at this passionate outburst. "Charles Frohlick. The dead boy. Okay, Derek and he were friends. Charles decided that Manolo was checking him out, in a sexual way."

Messenger nodded, distracted now as he squinted down at someone passing by on the street. I followed the direction of his gaze. He was watching a girl, maybe seventeen years old, with auburn hair, long, wavy. The girl turned to look at something we could not see from our vantage point, and her face was clear in the spill of light from a doorway. Messenger had leaned forward, and now he retreated and could not conceal his disappointment.

"You're looking for someone," I said.

He did not answer.

"The girl Oriax mentioned. Ariadne."

Both of his fists clenched and still he said nothing. Silence stretched between us as he began again to walk quickly along the battlement.

Was Ariadne a French name? Was Messenger French as well? Did such things as nationalities even matter to him?

"Continue," Messenger snapped over his shoulder.

"Well . . . Charles was upset because someone teased him about Manolo. Someone teased him and asked, joking, I thought, if Charles was gay. That set Charles off but not to the point of being really angry. I mean, yeah, angry, but not crazy angry like he got later."

"And why did he become crazy angry, as you put it?"

I shrugged, frowned, scrolled back in my mind through what I had witnessed in the last hours of observing Charles's life. "Derek," I said. "He kind of . . . pushed it. At first he was teasing, joking, but he wouldn't drop it. Actually, he was the one who said they should teach Manolo a lesson."

Messenger nodded. He stopped walking. The sun was going down fast. Floodlights snapped on, illuminating the walls, the towers, turning the crenellations dark by contrast. We had come to a mounting tangle of towers and a square building, a sort of castle that grew out of the walls and lorded its grandeur over the walled village below as well as the town beyond the river.

"Derek egged him on. Pushed him," I said.

"Why?"

"I . . . I don't know."

Messenger turned finally to face me. The low, slanting rays of a setting sun put sharp edges on his features, concealing his eyes but lighting his cheekbones, the side of his nose, his lips.

He was good-looking, bordering on beautiful. And this particular light, picking out some features while obscuring others, did nothing to make him less attractive.

He would certainly have stopped conversation in any schoolroom he ever walked into. If he had ever walked into a schoolroom.

Had he? Had this . . . boy, though that word didn't seem anything like correct . . . had this boy once attended school? Had a home? A mother and a father? A room with favorite objects on a desk, and items of clothing tossed about so that his mother had to chide him and demand that he clean up the mess?

Had he taken out the trash? Pulled all-nighters to finish the homework he had procrastinated on? Had he gone to movies with friends? Played around on the internet? Gotten his learner's permit?

Was he even from the same era as me? Did he live in my time, or was he from some very different time and some place unimaginable to me?

All that I knew of him was that he was different from any person I had ever met or imagined meeting. But was that because of who he was, or because of *what* he was? Was it possible to be the Messenger of Fear and remain somehow normal? It was no idle question if I was somehow destined (or was it doomed?) to become the Messenger myself.

Was I odd enough to become him? Or someone like him? Would I inevitably become solemn and taciturn? Would my habitual flood of words slow to a trickle as this life, this experience, this power, took their toll on me?

"There is evil in the world," Messenger said. "It comes from within us, but there are times as well when it is . . . suggested to us."

"Like Derek did with Charles?"

"And in another way as Derek and Charles did to Manolo. That is the evil that calls for justice." He cast another longing look down at the darkening streets and said, "I can't spend any more time here. We have our duties."

"Who is Ariadne? Why would she be here?" I asked. But I didn't really expect an answer, and got none.

With no sensation of movement we were thousands of miles away, standing in a noisy, bright-lit gymnasium.

The bleachers were half-filled, but the kids and parents there were enthusiastic, shouting encouragement and occasionally cheering in a disorganized but sincere way.

Out on the polished wood floor two boys in spandex uniforms, heads encased in the insectile helmets used by high school wrestlers, circled each other, crouched, cautious. One was Derek.

Derek lunged, caught the other boy's leg, pulled, and then fell atop the boy as he squirmed out of the hold, reversed with a smooth twist, and locked his arms around Derek's shoulders.

The cheering fell silent. The referee's whistle was stilled. The boy on top went limp and Derek, imagining he had just gained advantage, swarmed out of his grip, threw his opponent down onto the mat, and only after nearly a minute realized that no one but him was moving.

Bewildered, he looked up. He fixed his eyes on me first, then, nervous, shifted to Messenger.

"Derek Grady," Messenger said. "You are called to account for your actions."

Derek looked left, right. It would almost have been comical, had I not known some of what awaited him.

"What's going on?" Derek asked. He disentangled himself from his limp, blank-faced opponent, and stood up. He looked all around and yelled, "Hey! Hey, people! Hey! What the . . ."

His words trailed away as he saw a yellow mist begin to seep between the bleachers, through the frozen crowd, along the raftered ceiling, across the polished wood floor.

"What is this?" he demanded of me, choosing me, I supposed, as the one more likely to be intimidated by his belligerence.

I did not answer. Neither did Messenger. I had already begun to adopt Messenger's solemnity, though it had not been a conscious decision on my part.

"Derek Grady, I offer you a game," Messenger said.

"Who the . . . What . . . Go away. Get lost. Creeps."

"If you accept the invitation to the game and lose, you will suffer a punishment," Messenger said. "If you refuse the game, you will suffer punishment. If you accept the game and win, you will be allowed to go on without any further interference."

"Are you threatening me?" Derek demanded.

"I am offering you a choice," Messenger said.

"Yeah, well, I have a choice for you, loser: take a walk or get your butt kicked. How about that choice?"

Messenger said nothing. He just waited.

Derek was nerving himself up for a fight. He threw out his chest and made a "Come on" gesture with his hands. Messenger did not respond in any way, not by look or gesture.

Derek stepped closer, hesitated, glanced around as if expecting someone to stop him, and then leaped at Messenger. He passed through or past Messenger and landed on hands and knees a few feet beyond.

Angry and frightened now, Derek rushed at Messenger's back, and again space warped so that no contact was made, and Derek found himself yet more angry and frightened. Now Derek swung a fist at

Messenger, which would surely have passed harmlessly by except that Messenger had apparently lost patience and, with a simple raising of his palm, caused Derek's legs to weaken and drop him to his knees.

"I offer you a game," Messenger repeated. "If you refuse to choose, then I will make the choice for you."

"Game? What game?"

"Do you choose to play? Answer yes or no."

"Ah-ah-ahh!" a female voice called out. "Don't be too quick to answer."

Oriax, halfway up in the bleachers, stood and sauntered down, legs a mile long, dressed in her third exotic outfit. I wondered if Derek could see her, but from the way his eyes widened, his jaw dropped, and his face flushed, I assumed the answer was yes.

"You don't need to play Messenger's little game," Oriax said. "You're a big, strong boy, aren't you? You're not a pansy, are you? Not like Manolo, right?"

Throughout this, Oriax never even looked at Derek, but she winked at me and grinned saucily at Messenger.

Messenger ignored her, spoke past her to Derek. "You might lose the game. But you might win."

"*Might* win," Oriax mocked. "How many win, Messenger? One in ten? And only if the Game Master is in a gentle mood. It's all rigged, Derek, don't listen to him." She leaned close to Derek and put her cheek within a whisper of his. Derek's eyes fluttered and for a moment I thought he might faint.

"Let him be, Oriax."

"You're not going to be pushed around by some pretty boy in a ridiculous coat, are you, Derek? Not a big, strong, manly guy like you."

Derek shook his head. "No."

"I mean, look at him. You're tougher than he is, aren't you?"

Derek wasn't so sure about that, but he nodded gamely while glancing warily at Messenger. "This is all some kind of trick."

"Exactly," Oriax purred. "A cheap magic trick from a boy who serves powers he doesn't even understand.

Isn't that right, Messenger? You quote the phrases, you summon in the name of Isthil, but you don't know what that really means, do you? Child, you are still very young. And now you bully and seduce this poor, blind girl here into taking over your burden."

I did not want to listen to her—I felt a need to be loyal to Messenger, though I could never have explained it logically. What loyalty did I owe he who was not to be touched?

"Be silent, Oriax."

Oriax moved away from Derek and closer to Messenger. She waved one long, black-nailed finger slowly back and forth, and in a singsong voice said, "No, no, no, Messenger, you don't have that kind of power. You don't dismiss me. I was old in the knowledge before you were spawned." Her sex-kitten voice had grown hard and edged with anger. "I am Oriax. You know what I am, and who I serve, and what powers I command, and you should remember your place, Messenger."

Messenger did not show fear, but neither did he

rebuke her. He listened, swallowed a rising anger, kept his arms by his side, and made no reply.

Oriax turned back to Derek. She snapped her fingers in his face as if waking him from a trance and said, "Tell him no. Tell him no, you won't play his game."

Derek then looked to me, confused, a silent question in his eyes: Who should I believe? What should I do? And all I could do was shake my head slightly in a weak acknowledgment that I did not know the answer.

Derek threw his shoulders back again, glanced at Oriax, his eyes lingering on her, then in a voice lower than his normal register said, "No. I won't play your game."

Messenger glared daggers at Oriax, who clapped her hands and laughed in delight. She grinned at Messenger and said, "He'll break like a dry twig, the brittle little boy. And the Shoals will have a new inmate."

17

The mist now obscured everything in the gym and everyone but Derek, Messenger, and Oriax. It was particularly strange about Oriax, for the mist treated her as physical objects so often treated Messenger: it avoided her. She ranged through the frozen spectators, looking at them curiously, sometimes tilting their insensate heads back to better see their faces. I could see only the individuals directly beside her.

Oriax was playful, taking a sip of one person's beverage, looking in another's pocket, reading the book of the girl off to one side. She was killing time, waiting, bored. But refusing to simply disappear. Clearly she expected something more entertaining soon.

Messenger looked at me as if sizing me up, weighing my abilities in the balance. He did not seem encouraged.

"Oh, come on, Messenger," Oriax called from across

the gym. "She has to surrender her virginity eventually."

That particular phrase got my attention, to say the least, but I assumed she was being metaphorical. Though with Oriax, how could I be certain?

Derek was annoyed at being ignored and, I suspected, unsettled by Oriax's sarcastic dismissal of him as a brittle little boy. He still followed her with his eyes, only managing to glance back at us from time to time.

I must admit that I did not see Oriax encouraging him in any way, but Oriax's mere existence was encouragement, I suppose. It crossed my mind, just for the most fleeting moment, that it would be a wonderful thing to spend just one day looking like her.

"We have reached a moment I might have preferred to delay a little longer," Messenger said to me, his voice as always so close to my ear. "It is called—"

"The Piercing," Oriax interrupted, her tone mocking. "The Piercing. The perfect blend of solemnity and un-self-aware sexual metaphor. There's a lot of that, Mara; you'll get used to it if you decide to stay with Messenger."

"If I *decide*? I was not aware I had a choice."

"Oh, there are always choices, mini-Messenger. Not now, not today, not for you. But there are always choices. Sooner or later. Poor stupid Derek there made one. The time will come for you to choose as well. But right now the time has come for you to penetrate the veil of Derek's mind, to intrude into his memories, and to find oh such exciting and terrible things."

Messenger let her speak but was clearly having difficulty controlling his mounting irritation. "It is called the Piercing," he said, "because you will pierce all of the subject's defenses and discover the true fear at the heart of him."

"It's a hell of a ride," Oriax said, wandering nearer, much to Derek's enjoyment. He had gotten over whatever sting he had felt from her snide remarks. "The Piercing, indeed."

"I don't understand," I said truthfully.

"I am called the Messenger of Fear. The punishment I inflict is raised from the subject's own mind. It is to be his worst fear. In order to know what that fear is, you must travel deep within his mind, his very soul. It can be . . ." He searched for the right word. ". . . disturbing."

Derek said, "She's not going inside anything."

"There are words to be spoken," Messenger said.

"What are you talking about?"

"An incantation."

"An incantation? Like a spell?"

"Stand behind him," Messenger directed, and I moved with uncertain steps to stand behind Derek. Derek had laughed and tried to thwart this by turning around, but his feet were as if they had been glued to the wooden floor.

"Hey!" he yelled.

"Closer, Mara. Put your left hand over his heart, the center of his chest."

To say that I did not want to touch any part of this loathsome boy would be an understatement, but now my curiosity was running well ahead of my caution. I wanted to know what this was, what it meant, this Piercing. So I complied. He squirmed but could not move more than a few hairbreadths to the left or right.

I felt his heart beating through his sweaty uniform.

"Now place your right palm against the side of his head," Messenger directed.

Feeling silly, I nevertheless complied and resisted the powerful urge to apologize to Derek for this intrusion on his personal space.

"I'd rather she did this," Derek joked nervously, referring to Oriax.

Oriax laughed. It was not a joyful sound. There was the sinister mockery of the hyena in her laugh. "Would you?"

"Yeah, you're like, so hot."

"Mmm. You have no idea," she said.

"Now, speak these words," Messenger told me. "By the Source. By the rights granted to the Heptarchy. By Isthil and the balance She maintains."

The incantation was at once ridiculous and ominous. Surely it was all nonsense, the sort of thing that sounded impressive but meant nothing. Was I to believe there was such a thing as the Heptarchy? The word just meant seven of something, but seven of what? And who was Isthil? He'd mentioned that name before, I was sure, and when he spoke the name, it was with reverence. But once more, curiosity would be my preferred vice, so I spoke the words.

"By the Source. By the rights granted to the Heptarchy. By Isthil and the balance She maintains. I claim passage to your soul."

At first there was no change. I was disappointed, thinking either that I had failed somehow or that the words were indeed meaningless. Derek's heart beat beneath my left hand. His temple flexed beneath my right. And then, gradually, so that for several seconds I could not be sure it was real, my left hand felt more than the muffled thump of his heart and began to feel rather the discrete muscular contractions within. I could feel the components of the heartbeat: valves closing as others opened; muscles contracting as others relaxed; the surge of blood squirting from the heart to fill arteries and push the blood to the lungs and brain.

I swear I almost felt the slick wetness of his heart, the rubbery tension of stretched muscle, the warmth of the viscid liquid within.

And at the same time I felt the fingers of my right hand seem to melt into his head, the gritty feeling of hair, the thin layer of flesh, the hard bone, like wet stone.

I tried to pull away, but my hands would not respond. I sent a panicked, pleading look to Messenger, but now the mist seemed to conceal all but the shadow of him. Muffled voices of Oriax and Derek, neither comprehensible except for the underlying emotion: her derision, his growing nervousness.

I felt myself spiraling, twirling, hands still locked on to Derek while my legs swung around in a wide circle. It wasn't real, I was certain of that, or as certain as I could be of anything in this new, altered reality. But I could not un-feel the sensation of spiraling, of whirling madly while all the while descending, falling like Alice down the rabbit's hole.

Below me, darkness was penetrated by flashes of lightning. I fell or the darkness rose, I'm not sure which, but soon it was as if I was in a silent lightning storm, where each flash illuminated nothing but the texture of the darkness around me.

And then I was no longer falling but walking, moving with arms outstretched, unable to find any solid object, a frightened, unsteady wanderer in a black cave. I became aware of a presence. At first it seemed as if it was pursuing me, but no, it was before me and I was pursuing it. It was darkness at the center of darkness, a hollowness in the fabric of the air around me, a vacuum drawing me toward it even as it withdrew from my questing fingers.

And then an electric thrill shot up my arms as I touched the dark form. I felt again the wet and heaving heart, the slick bone, and deeper still my hands traveled until I touched something invisible, a writhing beast, and I cried out but made no sound, and this cry of mine seemed to still the frantic contortions of this unseen monstrosity.

I felt it. It was not big, no bigger than a large cat or small dog. My fingers traveled over it, making out tendrils, craters, some surfaces slick and wet, others like scabs.

There was a crease in it, a slight indentation that I suspected went the circumference of it, and I knew, though how I knew, I could not say, that I was meant to pry the halves apart. In obedience to this instinct I dug my fingers into the crease, and to my surprise, it came apart with no more effort than I might have had to exert to split apart a cracked egg.

And then. And then. Oh, God, how can I put into words the brutal images that erupted from that split? I saw Derek fleeing, panicked, running in sheer mindless terror from a pursuer that could neither be glimpsed nor outrun.

I saw him lying flat, tied down to a crude wooden

table, as above him a nearly comically large hypodermic needle descended slowly, slowly toward his abdomen.

I saw him behind the wheel of a car, and a tractor-trailer hurtling toward a head-on collision.

There were snatches of imagery from movies, some of which I recognized.

There were images of one-armed men with chainsaws that I heard as stories told round a dying campfire.

I knew what I was seeing as I plowed helplessly through the haunted house of Derek's imagination. I was seeing his fears, his darkest terrors, the stuff of his nightmares, the things that had frightened him from earliest childhood until this moment.

And worse, far worse than seeing these things, I felt them. I brushed against them, and each new terror sent shock waves through me. They were like infections that, once touched, I knew I could never fully shake off.

And I knew then, oh, with such soul-deadening dread, that this was what I had felt from my brief contact with Messenger. I understood then that he had absorbed some part of the terrors of so many tortured, twisted minds. I understood that he had never, could never, fully erase them from his own consciousness and that these terrors had made his touch toxic.

And that the same thing was happening now. To me.

I don't know how much time passed as I dredged through the accumulated horrors of Derek's mind. Maybe no time passed at all. Maybe it was a thousand years. Time lost all meaning—what good was time, how could it be measured, when all you could think to do was to scream?

Slowly then, slowly the unbearable intensity weakened. Slowly, like a person rising from a nightmare to the light, I floated up and away from the awful beast, the beast that now closed, locking me out. I floated up and away, up and away, but nothing, nothing was forgotten.

I opened my eyes. Derek was before me, his back to me, my hands on his heart and head.

I looked past him and saw Messenger. He was pale, as always, but somehow more deathly now. His blue eyes met mine, and I saw within them the thing that kept me from hating him as I perhaps should: compassion.

I had traveled to a place he had often visited himself. He knew. He understood in a way that no other being could.

My voice trembling, weak, I said, "You did this to me."

He shook his head imperceptibly. "No, Mara. You did this to yourself. As I did it to myself. As my master before me did it to himself."

Gasping, I broke contact with Derek.

"Was it . . . fun?" Oriax asked, unable to conceal the cruelty of her curiosity. She licked her green-tinged lips as though she was savoring the lingering flavor of some delicacy.

"What is his fear?" Messenger asked me.

"I . . . There were so many." I closed my eyes, but that brought the pictures back to life, so I opened them again, wide, knowing that darkness was now my enemy and that what salvation and peace I could find was in light, even the sickly light the mist allowed me.

"There was one fear greater than all others," Messenger said, his voice soft but insistent. "There was one fear beneath all of the others."

"Yes," I whispered. "Yes. There was."

18

Derek was four years old when he first heard the story of the Maid of Orléans. He wasn't even part of the conversation; it was something he heard his older brother talking about to a friend after reading Mark Twain's *Personal Recollections of Joan of Arc* in school. Derek's brother relished, in the way that slightly sadistic older brothers have done since the dawn of time, the opportunity to frighten his little brother.

Joan of Arc was born in the small French town of Arc in the year 1412 during the Hundred Years' War between England and France. England was winning.

She heard, or believed she heard, the voice of God directing her to offer her services to the French army. Through a bizarre set of circumstances, and owing to the credulous superstitions of the time, Joan ended up being taken quite seriously. She became a bit of a rock star for the French, who were happy to seize on any inspiration.

Joan, acting largely on her own, rallied a group of soldiers and peasants and townsfolk and captured an English stronghold. Then another. And then she began to capture entire towns and was able to get the Dauphin—the French king-in-waiting—officially crowned.

Then things took a grim turn for Joan. She was captured by the English. The French abandoned her to her fate, and she was dragged before a trumped-up religious court, which found her guilty of heresy in part because she had worn men's clothing.

She was taken to the town square and tied to a tall pole, and dry wood was piled around and beneath her. The fire was lit.

Derek's brother had reveled in the details. The way the flames would at first have warmed her. The way the smoke would sting her eyes. The jeers and insults of the crowd. The way her clothing would have been the first thing to burn, the way it would have curled and smoked and fallen away, and by then the agony would have begun.

Blistering skin. A smell like crisping bacon. Unbearable pain. Gasping for breath as the heat baked the air in your lungs. Skin bursting open.

I told Messenger. I was sure, you see, that he would never inflict anything so inhuman on Derek.

At the start of my recitation, Derek tried to laugh it off. But he began to sweat. He began to lick his lips nervously. And as Messenger listened impassively, Derek began to interject. "No, that's not right. That's not right. No. No way."

His voice grew panicky. Oriax's eyes glittered with an emotion I could only guess at. Messenger just listened. Just listened and did not stop me.

"Okay, man, okay, you're scaring me," Derek said. "I'll play your game. If I win, I go free, right? I'll play your game. Let me play your game!"

"You have done well," Messenger said to me.

"I think he's scared now—I think he gets it," I said, pleading Derek's case.

"Yeah, yeah, I mean, just, like, just, just let me play the game!"

"Too late," Oriax purred. And then she began to sing in a low but very melodious voice. It was a song set to an ancient melody I knew, though I did not at that moment recall the name and only later retrieved from memory that it was called "Greensleeves".

She sang this:

What fool is this, who cries and frets,
As doom is fast approaching?
Who made his bed, now will lose his head,
While Messenger laughs at his screaming?

It seemed to be made up on the spot, the mocking lyrics coming to her a few words at a time.

Messenger had in his hands a black cloth. I don't know where it came from. It was rough-textured, felt perhaps, and when he drew it over his hair and pulled it down across his face, it was revealed to be a hood. Only Messenger's eyes were visible, blue lights shining from eye slits.

"In the name of Isthil and the balance She maintains," Messenger intoned, "I summon the Hooded Wraiths and charge them to carry out the sentence."

"No, no, no, man, I didn't do anything wrong!" Derek yelled. "I was just doing it because Charles, man. Charles! It was all him, I never thought . . . I was just messing around!"

It was the mist itself that seemed to form the two dark and hooded figures now taking shape before my eyes. They might have been men, might have been human, but no feature was discernible, no touchstone of normalcy. They were too tall to be truly human, more than seven feet tall: at least they were that tall from the trailing hem of their cloaks to the pointed peak. There were no holes for eyes; no fingers protruded beyond their capacious sleeves.

Then the mist withdrew and I was reminded that we were still in a gymnasium, that people still filled the seats, though they remained unmoving. The light was unbearably bright on those immobile faces, but around us, and centered on Derek, a shadow formed. It was not the mist—it was some unnatural extinction of light, as though an invisible force field had formed around us, bending light away, allowing only the faintest illumination.

One of the Wraiths raised his arms and, with a shattering noise of ripping and tearing, the wooden floorboards twisted loose from the nails that held them. They flowed in streams from the edges of the gym floor, revealing glue-stained concrete beneath. They flowed, noisy, clattering, and swirled around Derek's feet.

I had no choice but to step away or be swept off my feet. I felt a jolt of guilt. I was abandoning Derek, a bad person, an angry, malicious person, but still, for all that, just a dumb teenager.

He stood rooted to the spot, twisting this way and that but unable to flee.

The wood piled around him, and some of the boards rose to a vertical, gathered together to form a stake, maybe eight feet high. And now Derek was rising as boards forced themselves beneath his feet, forming a rude platform.

The second Wraith made a graceful gesture of his arm, and cords that had held suspended banners released the banners to flutter away while snaking down as if they had come alive to wrap themselves around Derek and tie him to the stake. He was bound at the ankles, the knees, the thighs, the waist, the chest. His hands were unbound, but a rope circled his throat and held him to the pole.

"No, stop it! Stop it! Oh, God, stop it!"

That was not just Derek crying for mercy but me as well—this could not happen, this could not go on. Yes, Derek had caused a death, yes, he had ruined Manolo's life as well, but this was impossible, this was not tolerable. My insides were twisting, twisting as Derek screamed now, screamed, no longer able to plead, no longer able to form words, for sheer terror owned him now.

His eyes bulged, his chest heaved, and he screamed again and again as both Wraiths raised high their arms and flame grew from the ends of their sleeves.

"Messenger! No! No! No!" I cried, and I rushed at him, to beat at him with my fists, but I found I could not get near him.

Oriax was singing still, an eerily pretty voice carrying the ancient tune, but with words from no language I had ever heard before. There was a dark malice in the very sound of those words, an evil that did not rely on meaning but could be heard in the few vowels and the thick, clotted consonants.

The Wraiths lowered their flaming arms, and bright-yellow fire flowed like a liquid to touch the piled wood. The flames were bright in the pool of iniquitous darkness, and I prayed, while sightless men and women and children in the bleachers sat immobile.

I wish that I could have turned away. I wish that what came next never imprinted itself on my memory. I did not want, do not want, to know what fire does to a human body.

There was little smoke at first, though the burning varnish made an acrid smell. For the first few seconds Derek seemed amazingly unharmed. But then the hair on his legs singed and curled and fell away. The flesh of his legs reddened. His wrestling uniform shorts billowed out as hot air made balloons of them, and then, suddenly, they caught fire, curling up from the hem.

Bare flesh went from the red of a sunburn to something purplish and then black as the fat beneath the skin sizzled and popped like eggs on a too-hot grill. The skin burst open, like time-lapse video of rotting fruit. There was a nightmarish hissing, whistling sound as superheated gases escaped. Steam rose from flesh turned molten, flesh that ran down like rivulets of lava.

And yet Derek lived.

He had been screaming all along, but there is a difference between the scream of terror and the scream of agony. The raw sounds tearing Derek's throat were animal noises, not human. He bleated like a goat. He squealed like a pig. His mouth drew in air that instantly seared his throat and caused his lungs to begin filling with mucus, so that what were roars and screams and shrieks became grunts, mindless, choked animal grunts.

Derek's hair caught fire and for a moment his head was wreathed in smoke. I saw his leg bones were appearing as the muscle and fat melted away, white bone at first, then blackened, as his skin was blackened.

And still he lived. His body jerked frantically, spasms so powerful I wondered that his body did not tear itself apart.

"That's enough," I said through gritted teeth. "That's enough! Enough! Enough! *Enough!*"

But it did not end. Derek was a torch. It was no longer a simple wood fire; it was a fire of shreds of clothing, hair, and human grease. Flesh was melting away, revealing the structure of bone beneath.

And now more than ever: the smell. The contents of his stomach and bowels burned and stank like a sewage treatment plant. The meat of him burned and smelled like an outdoor barbecue.

It was the smell, the realization that with each inhalation I was drawing the atoms of Derek's body into my nose, the stink of human waste blended with a smell that to my horror made my stomach rumble hungrily, that sent me over the edge.

At the end Derek's eyes boiled in their sockets and, mercifully, I lost consciousness.

19

When I opened my eyes again, I was on the floor, sitting in a heap, collapsed as if my spine had been removed. My first conscious sensation was smell. Derek smelled like burned hamburger.

Then, all at once, the charred wood was made whole. All at once it was all back where it belonged, neatly covering the floor.

There was no stake. There was no more smell of charring flesh except in memory. The pool of darkness dissipated.

Derek lay crumpled on the floor. There was no mark of the flames upon him. His silly wrestling uniform was dark with sweat, but not with smoke or the stain of rendered fat. His hair was not curled from singeing. His eyes had not liquefied and sizzled down his cheeks.

He breathed.

He lived.

Oriax was still with us. She had ended her song.

Messenger had removed the hood from his head, and what he had done with it, I could not say.

"You are alive and unhurt," Messenger said. "Your penance is complete. The imbalance has been repaired. You are free to go."

I could only stare in disbelief. Unhurt? He had been burned alive. Or so it had seemed to me, and very definitely so it had seemed to Derek. This was justice? This atrocity?

The three of us waited, eyes all on Derek, ears straining to hear if he had any response.

I heard a sound like nothing that should ever have come from a human throat, yet it came from Derek. An eerie, low-pitched keening, repeated over and over again.

I went to Derek—I could not do otherwise—I crawled to him, touched his head, but he jerked away from me and raised a face utterly transformed by madness. His eyes were no longer human but like the eyes of a beaten dog near death, full of pain and incomprehension.

"Derek, it's over. It's over. You're not burned. It's over."

He began rocking back and forth, resting on one haunch, legs twisted together, his face in one elbow while the other arm just flapped like it was boneless.

"Like a dry twig," Oriax said.

"You're both despicable!" I raged at Oriax and Messenger.

"Yes," Oriax said, "but at least I have some fun with it."

Derek rocked, back and forth, back and forth, all the while keeping up his unearthly keening.

"The Shoals for him, then," Oriax said.

"That is not for you to decide," Messenger said tersely. Then in a voice that was flat he said, "Daniel."

Just that. He didn't yell it or speak any incantation. And Daniel was there.

Daniel glanced at Oriax and said, "I imagine you've done your damage, Oriax."

"Mmm," she answered. "Well, I sense that I am not wanted here." She winked at me and disappeared.

Daniel didn't seem to need any explanation, and Messenger didn't offer one. He knelt beside me, in front of Derek, and laid his hand on Derek's head. This time Derek did not flinch. I don't believe that Derek felt Daniel's touch, or that he felt or saw or heard anything at all anymore.

Tears were running freely down my face, and I felt so very sick and so utterly weary. But slowly I became aware that Daniel was looking at me.

"It was awful," I muttered.

Daniel nodded.

"He is a monster," I said, pointing a finger at Messenger. "He's a wicked, sick, sadistic monster."

Daniel waited to see if I was done, but I had no more words, just tears and sadness.

"Do you imagine that he enjoyed it?" Daniel

244

asked me. "Do you still not understand that what the Messenger of Fear does, he is *bound* to do? He's not a monster, he's a servant. And a penitent. Like you."

That word penetrated. *Penitent.*

"This is Messenger's punishment," Daniel said. "As it is yours. Each horror that he sees is a scar on his soul, a whip on his flesh. As it will be to you when you are the Messenger."

"Just a kid," I said, speaking about Derek but, I suppose, about myself, too. And even Messenger.

"Charles, too, was just a kid, and now he lies dead. And in a few weeks Manolo will be dead after hanging himself to escape the misery of his new life. Two dead, because of Derek."

I didn't want to argue with Daniel. I didn't have the strength.

"This isn't fair, this isn't justice," I said. "People do bad things all the time. They get away with bad things all the time. Why this one person? Why did we subject Liam and Emma to the test and risk this? Who knows what fears they may have had? And why Kayla, no matter how bad she may be? What horrors are you going to inflict on her?"

Daniel glanced at Messenger and might have been almost irritated. Maybe that Messenger had not explained these things to me. But then he nodded to himself, accepting it. He said, "Mara, we right the balance. Do we always right the balance? No. So we focus on . . ." He stopped, frowned thoughtfully, and said, "On what do *you* think we focus? Why are we dealing with these three cases? As you say, there are thousands of awful deeds every day. Why these three?"

"I don't know," I said.

"First," Daniel said, "they are young, and might do terrible things again and again if uncorrected. But I will tell you that had Liam and Emma merely run into a dog, the Messengers would not be involved."

"So, why?" I asked. I was not in the mood for twenty questions. My heart was a pain in my chest. My mind was unfocused, overwhelmed by the horror I had witnessed. They both waited then, like teachers waiting to see whether a dull student had grasped the lesson.

"Can't you just tell me? Can't either of you just explain?" I asked wearily. When they didn't reply, I groaned and dug deeper. "I don't . . . Unless it's that they each knew. That they had already seen what happened when they . . ." I felt my brow crease with concentration, felt as well the excitement of groping toward understanding. "It's that they knew. They each had a chance to stop. They didn't blunder into it, they didn't accidentally do something terrible, they *knew*. Is that it? Liam and Emma could have saved the dog but didn't. Derek and Charles had already been sent to detention and counseling. They knew what they were doing was wrong. And Kayla knew as well. She knew Samantha was struggling just to hold on. She knew what she was doing." I looked pleadingly at them. "Is that it?"

Messenger and Daniel exchanged a significant look. Daniel's had a nearly but not quite undetectable air of "told you so" about it.

Messenger said, "The balance of this world is not upset by accident. It is not upset by those who blunder accidentally into wrong. Evil comes when those who know better, who have seen the pain they cause, nevertheless cause more pain. The drunk driver who has already had near misses and knows that sooner or later he will take a life. The thug who has already seen a victim's blood and goes searching for more. The liar who has already destroyed a life and feels empowered by that ability to destroy. Those are the people who must be confronted. It will become a hunger for them, a need to cause and witness pain. Having done it once and escaped punishment, they will be drawn to it again. Each case had a chance to correct course, to learn and to atone and to move on. When they don't . . ."

"They may be visited by a Messenger," Daniel concluded. Then, lesson time clearly over, he turned his attention back to Derek. "Some learn. Some are destroyed."

"You burned him alive," I said. "Do you think

anything that you're saying justifies that?"

Daniel showed no reaction. But Messenger's pale face colored and he looked away.

"I will take him to the Shoals," Daniel said. "His mind is gone. The fear has broken him. But the day may come when he will find some peace."

Messenger nodded, stiff, avoiding my accusatory gaze.

"She needs rest," Daniel said, meaning me. "No more now, Messenger. And you as well, I think. Don't keep searching for her. Rest."

The second "her" was not about me, I thought, and that was confirmed when Messenger said, "A glimpse would be all the rest I would need. I had heard she was in Carcassonne. I performed my duties—I did what I must do. I just wanted . . ." But then, with a sigh that trembled coming out, he conceded. "I will rest, Daniel."

Daniel then did what I had thought no one could do. He laid a hand on Messenger's shoulder and said, "Not long now."

"Just tell me if she lives!" The words came out as a cry of pain, a pain I would never have believed Messenger capable of.

Daniel did not answer, but left his hand on Messenger's shoulder until the boy in black let his chin fall all the way to his chest in a pose of exhaustion and defeat.

Around us the room unfroze. Once again there were shouts and cheers and people eating nachos.

But there was no Derek. His disappearance must have seemed inexplicable. His wrestling opponent was looking around, baffled, the referee doing likewise.

I was done. Done with it all. Without asking permission or waiting for Messenger, I fled the room, passing through a heavy door that should have led to the outside but led instead to the room that was not my room and the bed that was not my bed, but was bed enough to catch my body as I collapsed.

20

I dreamed. Had I thought about it, I suppose I would have expected to experience nightmares. But I did not. Instead I found myself walking along a beach. There were tall buff-colored cliffs to my left. To my right, waves crashed and each time they did, the sound was a joy to me. A crash followed by all the sounds of suction drawing water back into the retreating wave like an inhalation. The sounds of pebbles rolling endlessly in the water, in and out, in and out, slowly, inexorably being ground down from rock to pebble to sand.

It was not hot, though the sun was in the sky, still well above the horizon. A stiff breeze blew the salt off the white foam, just cold enough to raise goosebumps from my exposed arms and legs. I looked down, in this dream, and saw that my feet were bare and coated in a layer of adhesive sand. I felt something in my hand and turned it palm-up to look at the half-dozen mismatched shells I had there.

I was happy. I could feel it. I smiled in the dream and smiled into my pillow.

The beach was a crescent, not very long, one of a dozen such small, hard-to-reach beaches along the coast north of Santa Cruz. In my dream I knew that's where it was. Santa Cruz. We went there sometimes. We. Whoever "we" was.

I looked down the beach and saw an old couple with low folding chairs, the man with a long-billed cap and sunglasses, the woman in the odd combination of down parka and sundress. No, they were not with me; I was not with them.

I looked back along the path made by my bare feet in the sand and saw a woman and a girl, maybe seven or eight years old. The woman was Asian, like me; the girl I couldn't see clearly enough to identify beyond the fact that she was wildly energetic, running in mad circles that cut through the white fringe of the crashing wave.

My mother? My sister?

I longed to run to them—it was foolish of me to feel that I needed time alone, off hunting for shells. Didn't I realize how much I would need them? How much I would crave their conversation, their still unremembered faces? I wanted to run to them, but even in the depths of the dream I knew I could not.

I looked up, craning my neck, bending my back, and shielding my eyes with my hand, to survey the top of the cliff. He was up there, the boy in black, Messenger. He had never been to this beach, I was sure of that, and the lucid part of me, the aware part of me that knew this was a dream and knew that I knew, felt his presence as an intrusion.

And yet I was not resentful. He was gazing out to sea, looking for her. For Ariadne, as if she could be out there somewhere. At that thought I turned to follow the direction of his gaze and spotted three surfers, two already paddling like mad to catch the wave that pursued them, while the third, a girl with auburn hair, sat astride her board waiting for something better to roll in.

I didn't call up to him, and he did not look down at me. I wondered if he was merely an image carried over from the day I had just endured, or whether he was actually present and aware inside my dream. Under normal circumstances that would never have occurred to me, but this was Messenger, and there was very little the boy in black could not do. He could freeze time and warp space.

And yet, I knew, he was as trapped as I was myself, as unable to escape. A fellow penitent.

I woke in darkness, rolled over, and stared up at the ceiling. What had Messenger done to earn this punishment? What did it have to do with the mysterious Ariadne? Was he even from my own time and space or was he a traveler from long ago or a long time yet to come? Was he the age he appeared to be, or was he older, maybe even much older? It was clear enough that I could not trust entirely the evidence of my eyes. This was a universe of illusion, of distortion and deception.

I thought of Oriax, pictured her, a beautiful young woman, but was she the mesmerizing, unforgettable, unequaled beauty I felt her to be when I was in her presence? Messenger had told her to let me go. Had she held some power over me?

What was Daniel? How had he known—if he did know—that poor Manolo was doomed? How had he known with a touch that Derek would be lost to sanity for at least a while?

What were the Shoals? And what, in the name of all that was either holy or rational, was this ridiculous Heptarchy and what's her name? Isthil.

I held my mind to these speculations for fear that, without a task on which to focus, my thoughts would veer toward darker, more awful things. Derek. Samantha Early. The fate that must befall Kayla.

No. *Had* befallen her.

That's what Messenger had said, though I wasn't sure I'd heard him properly when he said it. I strained to recall his exact words but could not get my fingers around them. Yet I was fairly certain, fairly, that he had said that whatever Kayla's punishment was, it had already been carried out.

This at least was a relief, for I could not imagine what buried fear I might find if tasked to enter her twisted mind.

Her motives at least I thought I could guess. Samantha Early had been a writer. So was Kayla, since she had the NaNoWriMo ribbon on her bulletin board. And if she was serious about it, if she saw herself as an author someday, she must have been devastated when Samantha Early, a girl Kayla despised as weak and weird, had suddenly shot from nowhere to publication.

Jealousy. That would have been it, or at least part of it. Jealousy coming at a time when Kayla was still coping with her father's death and her mother's renewed interest in the opposite sex. A time when Kayla would have been feeling vulnerable and alone despite her circle of friends.

That did not excuse the cruelty. Nothing excused, nothing ever could excuse, driving a girl to take her own life.

I wondered if Kayla had played Messenger's game or refused. Almost certainly she would have played. She seemed arrogant enough to imagine she would win. If she played, had she won? If she won, had she learned anything from the experience? Had she become a better person?

And if she had lost the game and faced the penalty, what had she endured? What was the terror she pushed way down into the darkest ratholes of her memory? What had she feared from the Messenger of Fear?

And with that I was dangerously close to asking that same question of myself: What was my deepest fear? How had I been punished for whatever wrong I was supposed to have committed?

"Food," I said to the darkness. "I am hungry."

I climbed from the bed that was not my own bed, used the bathroom, and showered, once more finding shampoo and conditioner and even the lotion I liked.

I looked at myself in the mirror. My face seemed unfamiliar to me, haunted by too much weariness, too much terror, too much guilt. I lived in a world now where nothing was as it had been, where nothing could be counted as set and certain.

I saw it all in my eyes, in the dark swelling beneath them that was so pronounced it almost looked like bruising. But even as I took that in, I was surprised by the way I looked, for the gauntness of my cheeks, the dullness of my normally glossy hair—always my best feature—the furrows beginning to etch permanent lines into my forehead, surely all these physical signs of stress had not manifested in just the short time I had been with Messenger. It occurred to me that my troubles in life might not have begun just forty-eight hours ago when I woke beneath the mist. And as I considered this, it became obvious that of course I must have been in trouble much earlier, else why would I have attracted Messenger's attentions?

"What did you do?" I asked my reflection. "What did you *do*, Mara?"

21

Messenger was in my kitchen. This fact was deeply unsettling to me, for I had come in a very short time and on the basis of very little evidence to imagine that this space, this false echo of my home or Kayla's home, or whatever this was meant to be, was mine and mine alone. I had thought it was a sanctuary. If Messenger could simply appear in the kitchen, then he could equally appear in my bedroom. And if all of that, then was I safe from Daniel or Oriax or whatever other beings may choose to intrude uninvited?

Messenger saw my annoyance.

"I'm sorry," he said. "I intruded."

"It's okay," I snapped. "I'm going to make some coffee if there is any coffee. Do you want some? Do you drink? Eat?"

"Coffee. Black."

"Of course black," I said.

I think he would have smiled then, had he been just a bit less *Messenger*.

There was coffee, a bag of it from Marin Coffee Roasters. I scooped it into the filter, added water, and started the machine running. Marin Coffee is my favorite coffee shop, and I sometimes go there after school to do my homework. . . . How did I know that? How had I, without trying, remembered sitting in that coffee shop? I could see it quite clearly. The front was often open to the fresh air. There were two rickety tables out on the narrow sidewalk, lots of tempting and fattening cookies and bars at the counter, a cooler in the corner, a bathroom at the back, big chalkboard menus high on the wall behind the baristas.

It was perhaps the clearest memory I had accessed, but it could hardly have been as familiar to me as my own home, none of which I could remember without confusing it with Kayla's house. Certainly I should have recalled my mother's face before I recalled a coffee shop.

The dream came back to me, the dream of the beach down by Santa Cruz, and I struggled to put it all in context. Samantha Early . . . Had she lived near me? Was I from northern California?

Oh, God. Did I know Samantha? Did I *know* Kayla?

The coffee machine sputtered its final drops and I poured into two cups, handing one to Messenger and looking for sugar for my own.

Messenger took a sip. It was the best confirmation I had yet had that whatever incredible powers he might possess, he was, in the end, human.

"Toast?"

"To what?"

"No, I mean I'm making toast. Want some?"

"Thank you, no," he said.

I dropped two slices of wholewheat bread into the toaster. I took my time about fetching butter and jam because I wasn't sure I was ready to face Messenger yet. I didn't know how to relate to him in these circumstances. He might be human, was human, but he was like no human I had ever met.

I wondered whether he had a place, like this one, a refuge where he went at the end of a hard day of torturing people in the cause of justice. I wanted to ask him, but at the same time I feared doing so, first because I thought it likely he would shut me down with his usual taciturn non-response. But also because part of me feared he might open up, tell me more than I wanted to know about him, and thus confuse even further my emotional reaction to him.

The odd thing, the thing that made me smile a bit wistfully to myself, was the realization that had he not been who and what he was, but just been a boy with that face and those eyes, sitting here drinking my coffee, I would probably still have been tongue-tied. I remembered so little about my own story, but I was certain that whoever I was, I had never been very good at making small talk with boys.

And then, as I spread butter onto a piece of toast, I saw it.

"What is this?" I stared aghast at the ink, blue and red, yellow and green, on my right arm, just above the end of my blouse sleeve.

I had caught only a hint of color peeking out, and now, without setting down the butter knife, I pushed my sleeve up to see it fully.

It was a tattoo. There was no swelling, no sense that this represented something applied by the usual methods within the last few hours. It was there, complete, healed, indelible.

It showed a boy, tied to a stake, with flames roaring around him.

"What . . . What is this? What is this? What have you done to me?"

I spun around, dropped the knife from numb fingers, held my sleeve up so that he could see it, pushed it toward him. I was torn between rage and a sadness at what felt like defilement.

I looked again at the tattoo. It was vivid, not quite real but still so detailed that it would never be mistaken for anything whimsical. It was the tattoo a sadist, a sick person, might have chosen and even then come to regret.

"What have you done to me?" I demanded as anger won out over sadness.

"It is not my doing," Messenger said. There was sympathy there but not much, and no surprise at all.

"How did it . . . When . . . Why? Why?"

"All Messengers of Fear are marked in that way," he said.

"It's sickening!" I cried.

"It is meant to be."

"But why? What is the purpose?"

He took a deep breath and a slow sip of coffee. He stood up and I thought at first he meant to walk away. Instead he shrugged off his long coat and laid it over the back of his stool. Then carefully, taking his time, he began unfastening the buttons of his storm-cloud-gray shirt. When he had unfastened them all, he slid the shirt off.

He had a stronger chest than I expected. His stomach was flat and muscular. His arms were lean and, if not gym-rat big, were nevertheless respectably powerful. But those were all observations I would make at a later time, for at this moment, when he stood naked from the waist up, I saw my own terrible fate.

He was covered in tattoos of pain and horror.

It was all the awful, shattering, mind-numbing scenes that touching him had sent flooding into my mind. Screaming faces with bulging eyes and mouths so distorted they looked scarcely human. Twisted limbs, some so attenuated that they seemed barely attached and maybe were not. Blood, in drops like sweat and in streams and in spouting fountains. Sharp objects, ropes, guns, drowning water and roasting flames, whips and chains and medieval instruments of arcane construction but manifestly foul purpose.

All of it inscribed on his body.

I stared and he allowed me to stare without comment, without explanation, without seeking to soften the blow. I knew this was what he had come to show me. He had known what would be done to me, and he had known that when I found that despicable art emblazoned on my own flesh, that I would be so destroyed by the vision of my future that I might not be capable of going on.

I was to be slowly, inexorably turned into a tapestry of retributive justice, if justice this was.

He slipped his shirt on, buttoning as carefully as he had unbuttoned minutes before.

"Why?" I asked, no longer capable of the energy required to shout.

He finished dressing, and then he said, "The world, Mara, the world you knew, that I knew, the world we saw as the only world, rests on the edge of a knife extended out over a sea of flame. Tilt to one direction, and fall into the flame. Tilt the other direction, and the same fate awaits. Lose our balance even a little, and slip onto the blade itself and be eviscerated."

"What are you talking about? Balance? What—"

"There are forces that badly want us to lose our balance. And there are countervailing forces that would see us maintain our precarious stance and survive. We, you and I, are tools of that second force. The task we are given is one small part of maintaining that balance."

He took a sip of coffee, finishing the cup.

"Those are just words," I said.

"Balance is everything," he said, almost in a whisper, though as always with Messenger, I heard his every word as if it were spoken by lips pressed against my ear. "The balance between good and evil, between true and false, between pain and pleasure, between love and loss, hatred and indifference. However you name them, these balances are all that keep the world spinning."

He moved around the counter and came to me. For a moment I thought he might touch me, and such was the spell woven by his words and, yes, by the inexpressible feelings he evoked in me, that I wished him to. Instead he used one finger to gently lift the sleeve and reveal the terrible thing beneath. He looked at it, solemn, sad and solemn, and said, "We are given great powers, though we did not choose to have them. And with power comes hubris—overweening confidence, arrogance. These marks, these terrible artworks, are our humility. They provide *our* balance."

"I don't want to . . ." I was unable to go on for the tightening of my throat. Tears blurred my vision. All I could see was my own body, my very self, marred forever, made into a living nightmare. No one would ever be able to stand to look at me. I would have to spend the rest of my life covered, concealed, ashamed. I wouldn't be able to look in a mirror. I would never have a boyfriend, never get married.

I sobbed. I sat down on the tile floor, my back against hard kitchen cupboards, and sobbed into my hands. I don't know how long I sat like that, feeling hopeless, so absolutely hopeless. I had not cried like that since my father died. I was lost. I was destroyed.

After a while the wracking sobs stopped, though the tears kept coming in waves, lessening, renewing, seemingly endless. I just didn't care if Messenger heard me or saw me. I didn't care because I was nothing. I was a stupid girl without a memory, weeping on the floor of a kitchen in which I did not belong.

Only when I was drained of not only tears but hope and self-respect did the slightest glimmer of anything that was not black appear at the ragged edge of my thoughts.

He had survived it.

Messenger had been the Messenger of Fear for . . . I had no idea how long. But his chest, his stomach, his shoulders and back and tapered torso, had all been covered with tattoos of vile tortures, each the equal of mine, and perhaps the rest of him as well, and yet he lived. Yet he had not lost all humanity, I thought. Yet he still longed for his Ariadne.

Somehow the boy in black had survived, and, I was sure, still had hope.

Having hated him, raged at him, believed every foul thing about him, I nevertheless knew that he had hope. And I knew this because he had shown me. That was why he had taken me with him to Carcassonne. To show me that despite all the inconceivable fear he had witnessed and necessarily felt, still, he *hoped*.

My knees were stiff, my muscles sore, as I stood. Messenger was gone, but I knew I would find him.

I ate my cold toast, barely tasting it. I cannot say it restored all my strength, but it helped. Then I walked to the kitchen door, put my hand on the brass knob, took a shaky breath, twisted it, and stepped through to find myself once more outside Samantha Early's home, where Messenger waited for me.

"You have something to tell me," I said. "You've been preparing me."

For just a second, so brief that I could never have sworn it was real, though I wished fervently to believe that it was, he seemed to feel sorry for me. It was gone in an instant, replaced by his more usual expression. But the sense that he had pitied me, that he knew what was coming and pitied me, scared me.

"Yes," Messenger said.

"Then . . . I'm ready."

22

The end came despite well-meaning efforts to stop it. One of the parents heard about what was happening to Samantha at school and called Samantha's mother.

We were there at the aftermath, Messenger and me. Samantha's mother, a woman with thinning red hair and a weary, put-upon expression, found Samantha in the garage. The garage was like so many, a mess of folded lawn furniture, plastic bins of papers and old books, slumping cardboard boxes, a once organized, now haphazard peg board of tools. There was no car; the garage had obviously been turned over to use for storage.

A washer and dryer piled high with laundry.

Against one wall was a metal locker, red, closed with a combination lock.

"What are you doing in here, honey?"

Samantha looked up guiltily from the cardboard box she had been rummaging through. A small pile of objects sat on a table that had obviously once been used for arts and crafts, as it was spattered with paint and globs of dried glue and even scraps of tissue paper stuck in place. The objects included a tiny silver cup inscribed with words I could not see from where I stood. And there was what looked like a grammar school project, a storybook covered in construction paper and decorated with crayon drawings of a girl and a dog.

"Oh, I'm just, you know, looking for some stuff for my room," Samantha said, pushing the storybook aside self-consciously.

"I heard you're having some issues at school," the mother said.

"Issues?"

"Sam, are you being bullied?"

Samantha shook her head. "No, I'm fine."

"One of the mothers called me. Mrs. Jepson. She seemed to think you were being picked on."

"No, Mom, I would tell you."

"Would you? Because I can help."

"I'm fine, I'm just, you know, redecorating my room." She gestured at the stuff on the table. "I was looking for Miss Pooky."

"Who?"

"Nothing."

"Was that your bear? From when you were little?"

Samantha was embarrassed. "Yeah, I think so, wasn't it? Did you want something else?" Her eyes pleaded for her mother to go away. Her mother's eyes were worried but vague, and I saw the slight shrug and the surrender that signified the mother's acceptance of her dismissal.

After the mother was gone, Samantha searched for a while longer, before giving up on finding her bear. She went to the metal cabinet. She spun the combination, mouthing the numbers to herself as she did. The lock snapped open and, with a steadying breath, Samantha opened the metal door.

Inside, resting on their stocks, were a rifle and a

shotgun. On a shelf at the top of the cabinet was a soft, deerskin zipper bag and several greasy cardboard boxes of shells.

Samantha glanced anxiously toward the door through which her mother had emerged. She took the deerskin bag to the table, unzipped it, and folded it open, revealing the blued-steel gun within. She fetched a box of ammunition. It was a bit like a large matchbox, with an inner tray that slid open to reveal neatly stacked cartridges, brass and lead and smelling of oil and sulfur.

"Can't we stop her?" I asked, though I knew the answer. This had already happened. Hearing no response and expecting none to come, I posed a second question, a question tinged with bitterness. "Why do people have guns? Don't they know?"

"Her father thought he was protecting the family. And he thought it was safe."

"Then why did he tell her the combination?"

Messenger shook his head. "He didn't. She guessed it. Her birthday; month, day, year. This is not the first time that Samantha has taken the gun out to look at it, to think about it, to consider . . ."

Samantha counted out three shells. Three cylinders, like miniature fireplugs in shape, each no bigger than a little finger. Samantha stared at the shells and frowned. The number troubled her. The number was not right, not her number.

Her number was seven. She counted out seven shells, lined them up with excruciating care, servant even now to her obsessive–compulsive illness. Seven in a row.

She counted them by tapping each slug with the tip of her finger.

Then she counted them again. Again. Again. Again. Again. Again.

Seven times she counted until her demon could be satisfied. Seven times seven.

She popped the clip out with practiced ease and loaded the bullets in one by one. Each one made a multi-part click. When she was done, she slid the clip back into the handle of the pistol and piled the gun and her mementos into a crumpled brown paper bag. She walked away, shoulders slumped, tread heavy.

"I can't watch this again. We don't need to watch this again," I said.

"No," Messenger agreed.

Less than ten minutes later Samantha would fire a single round into her brain and die within seconds.

"Her mother . . ." I said, overcome with a wave of pity, guessing that she would play those last few minutes with her daughter over and over and over again in memory and in dreams. She would blame herself. She was blameless, but that would not stop her blaming herself and then her husband.

A question occurred to me, one that Messenger might even answer. "If she had tried to kill herself and survived . . . would she have been visited by the Messenger of Fear?"

"Should she have been?" he asked me.

I thought about it for a while, standing in that

gloomy garage. I don't know why, but it felt necessary to me, to think through what Samantha was about to do, what she had in fact already done.

"Yes," I said at last. "She has no right."

"She is a girl with a crippling mental problem who has been bullied," Messenger said.

"Yes," I agreed. "And Kayla deserves to be punished. A long and terrible punishment, because her bullying pushed Samantha to the point where she couldn't endure it anymore. But . . ."

"But?"

"But there has never been, and there never will be, a reason to take your own life."

"Because?" He was genuinely curious, I think. He was watching me as I answered, something he rarely did.

"Because mostly people live, I don't know, eighty years, whatever the number is. She's sixteen. She's lived a fifth of her life, eighty percent still to come. That's too early to declare defeat and surrender. People despair and yet go on, and many of them, maybe even most, have wonderful lives. College. Career. Love. Children, maybe, grandchildren, and giving up when you're sixteen?" I shook my head. "It's a sin. It's an awful, wicked, ugly sin."

There was a long silence between us. Then, through the floors and walls we heard a muffled *Bang!*

The silence stretched.

"A sin," I said, tears filling my eyes. "But I guess she's paid all she can pay for her sin."

"And Kayla?"

I brushed away the tears, even as I heard her mother's voice, worried, cry, "Sam? Sam?"

"I want to be away before she screams," I said, barely able to force the words through gritted teeth. "I don't want to hear her mother scream."

The garage dissolved into the school. It was morning, before the bell. The car line snaked down the street and through the parking lot. Kids jumped out of cars and vans and SUVs, reached in to grab backpacks, then rushed away to join friends or just head to the first class.

Inside, the arriving crowd was compressed into the main hallway of my school.

I stopped moving then. *My* school?

I looked to the left and saw a poster. The colors had changed since Messenger and I had visited before. Now they were green and white. There was a well-drawn caricature of a pirate with a cutlass clenched in his teeth. SIR FRANCIS DRAKE HIGH SCHOOL, HOME OF THE DRAKE PIRATES. GO GREEN.

"This isn't the . . . This is . . ."

Messenger said nothing, but I had the sense that he was standing just a bit closer to me than was his habit.

I felt for tendrils of memory. It was like trying to grab wisps of smoke. They were there, I could almost touch them, but when I tried, they slipped away, leaving only bits and pieces, impressions. They left a residue of emotion but without explanation.

And yet I knew this place. This school.

My God, had I known Samantha Early? Was I one of the many who must have known that she was in pain, must have known that she was being bullied?

The ground seemed to be moving beneath me, like a slow-motion earthquake. I felt nauseous, and as if that was only the merest symptom of a terrible illness that was coming my way, inexorable, impossible to sidestep.

"Where's Kayla?" I demanded. "That's what you've come to show me, isn't it? That's why we're here, isn't it? So where is she?"

The bell rang and the crowd, already thinning, evaporated with a loud banging of lockers, sneakers squeaking on fresh-waxed floor and the usual calls and jokes and promises to hook up later.

"Where is she? I want to see her. They're going to announce it, aren't they? They always do when there's something awful that's happened, they do, over the PA, Ms. Seabury, she'll . . ."

I was breathing hard, though I wasn't moving fast enough to warrant it. I moved with an ease I would have found impossible to believe days earlier, right through doors, into and out of classes, hurrying, searching faces for Kayla. AP Comp, that's where she would be, first period.

I was panting now, my heart pounding madly in my chest, hurrying, a blur as I passed through solid objects, a ghost in my old school, because yes, it was my old school, my school, and there was J.P., as usual, clowning in the back of the chem lab, and I knew him. I knew Alison DeBarge, twirling her hair sullenly over close to the window in French. They were both part of my circle of friends.

My group. My friends. They weren't the coolest of the cool, maybe, but the group around me, the ones who sometimes called me M-Todd.

M-Todd. Mara Todd.

M-Todd.

How had that gotten started, that stupid nickname? Someone . . . Shannon, yeah, it was her, Shannon, my best friend, who had come up with that and for some stupid reason it stuck, even though it was stupid, as stupid as K-Mack.

I stopped suddenly. Stopped and stuck out my hand to hold myself up against a wall that avoided my touch.

Dread. It was coming for me. I felt it looming behind me, before me, all around me. Dread.

"No," I whispered.

Messenger, knowing, waited. Waited, and I hated him for that patience, hated him for already knowing what I could only feel as a terrible beast coming to devour me.

"Where's Kayla?" I demanded.

And he said nothing.

"Where is Kayla?" I cried out. "Where is she? Where is Kayla? Where is Kayla?" My whole body trembled. I shook like I was seized by fever chills.

"Where is Kayla?" I screamed.

And only then did Messenger say what I knew he must say. "There is no Kayla."

23

Something inside me broke. Can a soul break? I was hollowed out. I was nothing.

"No," I pleaded.

And he said nothing.

"No," I begged again.

"Mara . . ."

"No," I said, but flat now, knowing at last that the moment had come for truth. Still, though, I bargained for some better answer, any other answer besides what I now felt as truth. "I saw her. We both saw her. We both heard her, Messenger. She has blond hair." I grabbed a handful of my own black hair and held it out as evidence. "She's white, I'm Asian. She's . . . not me. Not me."

"You were not ready for the truth," Messenger said. "I hid it from you, with illusion and misdirection. With the face of a girl who looked nothing at all like you. You had things to learn first. You had things to understand. First."

"Did I miss it? Am I too late?" Oriax. She was there, this time dressed head-to-ankle in a shiny black leotard. I looked down and saw that she no longer wore boots to cover her too-small feet. I saw there the truth, the glossy black hooves.

She was bending down to bring her face level with mine. "Oh, good. Oh, such lovely tears," she said. She licked her green lips. "I would lick them off if Messenger would let me. Delicacies to be savored. The tears of remorse." She shuddered like a person fantasizing about some imagined pleasure. "I'll bet they are ever so bitter."

"Leave me alone," I said, my voice weak, my whole body sick and unsteady.

"Alone?" Oriax mocked. "Oh, little mini-Messenger, you have so much still to learn. You and I are going to be BFFs. Sooner or later, you'll break, little girl. And I will laugh as you are carted away to the Shoals. Shall I tell you about the Shoals? Would you like me to show you around that happy, happy place? You'll end there eventually."

She laughed. It was a sound full of glee and madness, rage and lust. But it faded mercifully as the scene changed again. The school was gone, as was Oriax. I felt a chill breeze on my face. There was salt in the air. I knew even before I looked that I was on that beach, the one from my dream. The one from my memory.

We were alone, Messenger and me. The sand crescent was abandoned, and the sun was dropping toward the horizon, touching the thin clouds with fire.

Messenger did not rush me. He asked nothing and said nothing, content to wait. He knew what I would have to say, the words that would be wrung from me as though by some terrible torture. And finally, I said them.

"I killed Samantha Early."

He did not speak, but he had heard, and he then released the last of his hold on my memory.

My name is Mara Todd. My birthday is July 26. I was born in the maternity ward of Tripler Army Medical Center in Honolulu. My father had been stationed there at the time.

We had moved around, like many military families. I had lived in Hawaii, Virginia, the panhandle of Florida, and when my father was deployed overseas for the last time, we moved to San Anselmo, California, because it was near where my paternal grandparents lived. My mom and dad thought it would be good for me to be close to family for a change.

Middle school had been hard for me, but when we moved to San Anselmo, I found a place for myself at Drake. It was a humane school. San Anselmo was a good place to live. Steep, wooded hills in the shadow of Mount Tamalpais—Mount Tam, to everyone who knew it. We were just north of San Francisco and south of wine country.

I had liked it immediately, and loved our house above the creek, hidden away in the trees. We'd been happy there, me, my little brother, my mom, and when he could get away on leave, my dad.

Then he had died. And that was when I began to feel that I had stories to tell. That was when I started to feel the urge to write. My teachers praised me. It was what I had that made me special, a talent.

And then, Samantha Early had leaped past me. Suddenly Spazmantha was the real thing, a soon-to-be published author, and I was . . . a kid with promise.

"I was jealous," I said.

"Yes," Messenger said.

"I knew. Did you see that when you looked into my soul? That I knew Samantha was troubled? I had seen her washing her hands, I'd observed her doing counting rituals. I knew she had a problem. I knew what it was called. I knew how serious it was."

For once I was grateful for his silence.

"I knew and I used it. I knew what I was doing

was wrong. I was mad at my mom for . . . I guess, for going on with her life. I was mad at the world for taking my dad. I couldn't stand that . . . that I should lose him, and then lose the one thing I had come to care about. I did just what you said. I knew. I *knew* what I was doing."

I listened to the waves. I breathed deeply of salt air.

"There's one thing missing from my memories," I said.

"Yes."

"I need to see it."

The beach faded as the mist flowed from the water, from the sky, from the sand beneath my feet.

I was alone. I had been alone. Back when the mist had first come for me.

"What the . . . Is this fog? What is—" I had stopped talking then when I glimpsed a figure coming toward me from that sickly yellow mist. I had squinted to see clearly, to discern first the shape and then the detail of that gaunt, pale face framed by long black hair.

I had noted the coat, the shirt, the boots, the buttons of death's heads. The rings on his hands, one a symbol of life, the other a representation of agony.

I had looked into the blue eyes, searching for an explanation. And he had said to me, "I am the Messenger of Fear. I offer you a game."

He had explained my very limited options to me. I could choose to play the game, and if I won, I would go free. And if I lost, I would be punished for my deeds. I would be scourged for the death of Samantha Early. I would endure my worst fear.

I had chosen to play the game. It had been grueling, all but impossible. I had been made to cross a desert wasteland and tasked to collect seven objects that would be visible, but just barely.

Seven objects, scattered on sun-blasted rocks and barely peeking out from rattlesnake holes.

A pen.

A pad of paper.

A combination lock.

A folded flag.

A gun.

A skull.

A tattered brown teddy bear.

There had been no time limit set, except that hunger and thirst applied their own unique pressures. It had taken me many hours, or at least I had experienced them as hours. Hours of wandering beneath a blistering sky, denying as I walked that I understood the significance of the objects.

But when I was done, when I held all seven objects in weary fingers, I knew.

Memory faded away and I once again beheld the beautiful Pacific, the waves gentling now as the sun turned all the world pink and orange and gold.

"I won the game," I said.

"Yes," Messenger said. "You were free to go. You did not."

I shook my head, recalling that last as well, but

Messenger told it to me as if it was a story I had never heard.

"I told you that you had won. That you were free to go on. And you said, 'No.' That you did not deserve to walk free. That you deserved to be punished."

"Daniel was there," I said.

Messenger displayed one of his rare, fractional, fleeting smiles that never quite became a smile. "Daniel generally is."

"He said he had a way. He said it was not a punishment he could impose, but rather one I could choose to accept. But once I accepted—"

"You would be bound. You would be bound until your penance had been completed."

I nodded. I wondered if Messenger had come to this same duty by a similar path. I believed he had. I doubted he would ever tell me the how and the why of it, but in that I proved to be mistaken. It would be a long time coming, but in the end I would know all.

"I am to be the Messenger of Fear," I said, and my

voice no longer quavered as I spoke, though this terrible truth would have left me whimpering before.

"When you have learned," Messenger said. "When you are ready."

I suppose I should have been accustomed to sudden changes of venue, but it still came as a surprise when I blinked, opened my eyes, and saw that I was in a place like no place I had ever known or imagined.

It was both an open and a closed space, at once vast and intimate. I felt myself to be at the bottom of a well, a cylinder driven deep into the earth. Hundreds of feet, maybe even thousands. Looking straight up, I could make out a flattened circle of stars, and even the melancholy lights of a passenger jet miles above.

The sides of this well were lined with dull golden rectangles, each perhaps ten feet tall and half as wide. All that I could see—and most were too far above me to be seen clearly—seemed to have been inscribed in careful, ornate calligraphy.

There was no other visible source of light that I

could see, no lamps or sconces or torches. But there was a glow greater than could possibly have come from the cold stars, and of far warmer hues. It seemed almost that the gold itself was glowing softly.

The nearest of these tablets ended just above my head, and peering through the gloom at this, I read names. Some were easily recognized: Tom, Harley, Diana. Others were more exotic: Akim, Shadan, Caratacus. Some were in Western script; others appeared to be Chinese or Japanese, Arabic or Hebrew. There must have been thousands of names. Maybe tens of thousands.

While the well was basically circular, one wall was flattened, and on this wall no golden tablets glowed. Instead there was a hugely tall painting, or perhaps what is called a fresco—paint saturated into fresh plaster. I could see only the bottom of it clearly but still had the impression of three distinct sections.

One was a sort of group portrait, seven strong and proud people in flowing robes, their heads wreathed in a yellow mist, almost like a halo.

The second was a single female figure. She was tall, dressed in armor, with a leather skirt and greaves on the legs and arms. She held a short sword in one hand and hefted a shield with the other. She did not look as if she were pretending to be a warrior. She looked like she'd been born a warrior.

"You gaze upon the picture of Isthil, goddess of justice and wickedness."

"I thought it might be," I said. "This is old."

"This place was old before the first pyramids," Messenger said.

"Isthil is one of the seven in the other portrait," I said.

"Yes. The Heptarchy, seven gods given dominion over the affairs of man, in service to the Source. Estrark, goddess of harvest and hunger. Gabril, god of flesh and spirit. Ash, god of peace and war. Yusil, goddess of creation and destruction. Ottan-ka, god of pain and joy."

"Isthil makes six," I pointed out. "Who is the seventh? The beautiful . . . well, I can't tell if it's male or female."

"That is Malech. Malech is neither male nor female, for Malech is the god of pleasure and denial. Malech . . . well, you must understand that there is no peace between the gods. Some have retreated from the world, no longer necessary. Some are true to their calling. But Malech, and Ash, too, have turned against man."

"Oriax," I said, realizing it even as I said it. "She's Malech's messenger. As you are Isthil's."

Messenger didn't speak, leaving my statement to stand as truth.

"The last picture. I can't even . . . It's just a sort of sun, or star, or . . ." I frowned. The image of the Heptarchy and the portrait of Isthil were both realistic pictures within the limits of an earlier artistic sensibility. This last was abstract—symbolic, perhaps.

"The Source," Messenger said.

"And what is the Source?"

"The ultimate balance, more important than any other. Each of the gods maintains a balance between ends of a spectrum. Harvest and hunger. Creation and destruction. But the essential balance that transcends every other is between existence and nonexistence. Existence is not a simple thing. It takes work. It takes balance. In our small way, we labor to maintain the balance."

This was without doubt the most words Messenger had ever spoken to me. I understood that his willingness to answer questions was because an important lesson was being taught. This was school. I was determined to get all from him that I could.

"Where are we?" I asked Messenger. "This place."

"This is the Shamanvold. Here on these gold tablets are written the names of all the Messengers who have served Isthil and the balance She maintains."

I tore my attention from this overpowering display to look at Messenger. He gazed up with an expression of profoundest respect. But that respect was not simple awe. This was not worship. Rather he seemed moved and determined, but also terribly sad.

They had buried my father at Arlington National Cemetery. It is a sacred place with its row upon row of stark white marble markers, each testifying to a man or woman who has died in service. Everyone there had been sad and reverent and respectful as they lowered the casket into the ground. But I had looked past our own funeral, past my mother and my relatives, and I had focused on the face of a very old man, an old soldier who was no part of our ceremony. He was a man who was not just seeing but remembering, knowing in his bones and to the depths of his soul what the place represented. Such sadness. But pride, too.

I was looking at that old soldier as the honor guard fired their rifles for my father. He had looked up then, seen me watching him, and raised a feeble hand in salute.

MICHAEL GRANT

I saw now a reflection of that same sadness and pride on Messenger's much younger face. Messenger wasn't a visitor to this place—he was part of it, part of whatever it represented. He understood, in a way that I did not, what we both were seeing.

"One day, when my service is done, my name will be inscribed here. And yours," Messenger said. "Then we will each face a choice." He didn't elaborate, and I could see his briefly open expression closing down.

"I don't understand it all," I admitted.

A sound came from him then that I would not have thought possible: he laughed. "Nor should you, yet. As I said, not everything can be taught. Many things must be lived." He cocked his head, looked at me appraisingly, maybe even with a glimmer of affection, and said, "Enough for now. Pain is balanced with joy, and it is time you learned something about that. There are small joys and compensations in this duty we perform."

"Joys?" I was incredulous. If there were joys to be

found in this doom I had chosen, I failed to guess what they might be.

"Come," Messenger said.

24

Something was odd about the house. For one thing, it was distinctly southwestern in flavor, with thick adobe walls of a soft ochre color. The floors were dark hardwood, the lights soft, and then I realized why it struck me as so strange. The walls were not, in fact, thick adobe; on closer examination, they were glass panels and the ochre look was a projection. A very convincing projection that came from no source I could discover.

We passed into a dining room, where a family sat. Two children, both girls, sisters by their features but at the same time charmingly different. One had red hair and a pale but sunburned complexion. The other was Latina, I imagined, for her coloration was right at home in this decor. The first girl was four or maybe five, the other a tween.

They were eating pizza, and I am ashamed to admit

that the sight of the pepperoni caused a hunger pang in my neglected belly.

It was easy to see how the girls had come by their different appearance, for their parents, a mother and father, were older images of that same dichotomy, one pale, one dark.

The father said, "Did we not get red pepper flakes? I don't like it unless it's spicy."

The older girl flicked a package to him, which landed on his plate. He chided her, but everyone laughed.

The mother said, "Yes?" It was the "yes" you use to answer a phone, although if there was a phone, it was so small as to be invisible. Then, with a resigned sigh, she said, "Twenty minutes."

"Oh, come on," the father moaned. "You have to go?"

"I'm indispensable," the mother joked as she stood up. "Girls, don't drive your father crazy—I have to go to work."

There was something familiar in her voice, then

in her face, and then it fell into place.

"Is that . . ."

"Liam and Emma. In twenty years," Messenger said.

"Where is she going?"

"She's on call," he said. "She's a doctor. A veterinary surgeon."

I smiled, and then my smile faded as I remembered another poor penitent. "And what about Derek in twenty years?"

Messenger was silent for a long time. At last he said, "Take what joys come, Mara. They will be few."

"Where is he, Messenger? Where is the boy whose mind we broke?"

"He is at the Shoals."

"And what is that?"

He shrugged. "A prison. A hospital. A sanctuary. It is what its residents make of it. A last chance to find his way back to sanity."

"Just tell me one thing, Messenger," I said. "Just tell me that you know it was too harsh. Tell me that you know that we did wrong while trying to do right." He was silent, so I tried one last time. "Tell me that you will cry for Derek."

He said nothing. He didn't even look at me. But I saw tears in his eyes. He clenched one hand into a fist and pressed it against his heart, and nodded so slightly that I could have doubted I'd seen it.

But I did not doubt.

"One more question and I will leave off. You created the illusion of Kayla. You created a face to conceal my own. Whose face was it, Messenger?"

He didn't answer, and I didn't really need him to. The color of the hair was different, but he had used the face of his beloved Ariadne.

Small joys and compensations.

We stood there, unseen, watching as Liam and Emma's family argued over who would get the last slice. Then Messenger said, "It's time to go."

"Where?" I asked.

"To do our duty."

We left the house and were somewhere very different, ready to witness, ready to offer, ready to punish, to keep the balance of the world.

To be the Messengers of Fear.

Acknowledgments

Every book is a collaboration. I'm lucky because my collaborator-in-chief, Katherine Tegen, is also my smarter, wiser friend. Through her I am incredibly fortunate to have the help of Kelsey Horton, Kathryn Silsand, and Jennifer Strada, Joel Tippie and Amy Ryan, Raymond Colon and Lauren Flower and Casey McIntyre. We had fun creating this book. We all hope you had fun reading it. More are coming.

I'm on Twitter as @TheFayz. I can't answer every tweet, but I read them all, and I love hearing from you, because you are the final element of this collaboration. Once I'm done writing it, the story is yours.

Thanks.

—Michael Grant

Discover the number 1 bestselling series from Michael Grant

299 HOURS 54 MINUTES

A small town in southern California: In the blink of an eye everyone over the age of 15 disappears. Cut off from the outside world, those that are left are trapped, and there's no help on the way. Chaos rules the streets.

Now a new world order is a rising and, even scarier, some survivors have power – mutant power that no one has ever seen before . . .

'I love these books' Stephen King

HAVE YOU GONE BZRK ?

A GLOBAL WAR IS RAGING
YOU CAN'T SEE IT
IT'S HAPPENING INSIDE YOU
AND IT CHANGES EVERYTHING

Michael Grant has always been fast paced. He's lived in almost 50 different homes in 14 US states, and moved in with his wife, Katherine Applegate, after knowing her for less than 24 hours.

Michael is the author of the no.1 bestselling **GONE** series and the groundbreaking **BZRK** trilogy. Michael and Katherine have also co-authored more than 100 books, including the hit series **Animorphs** and ultra-modern mystery thriller, **Eve & Adam**.

Michael, Katherine and their two children live in the San Francisco Bay Area, not far from Silicon Valley. Michael can be contacted on Twitter (@thefayz), Facebook (authormichaelgrant), and via good old-fashioned email (Michael@themichaelgrant.com).